# The Mystery at the Crystal Palace

As she entered the arena, Nancy glanced around the lobby in surprise. Yesterday the arena had been jammed with people. Today there was no one in sight. It was hard to believe a major competition would be taking place here in one day.

Moving to the main rink, Nancy saw that Amanda was the only skater on the ice. As she passed through the lobby on the way to Alison's office, Nancy watched Amanda practice her double axel while classical music played softly.

Suddenly the music stopped, and the Crystal Palace was plunged into darkness.

Nancy heard Amanda gasp. Then the roar of a motor filled the arena. Lights shone across the rink, capturing Amanda in their blinding beams.

Nancy couldn't believe her eyes. The huge Zamboni machine was bearing down on Amanda, but Amanda didn't move an inch. The glaring lights had caught her frozen in terror!

# Nancy Drew
# Mystery Stories

## Available from MINSTREL Books

# NANCY DREW® 133

## THE MYSTERY AT THE CRYSTAL PALACE

## CAROLYN KEENE

A MINSTREL® BOOK

Published by POCKET BOOKS
New York   London   Toronto   Sydney   Tokyo   Singapore

A MINSTREL PAPERBACK *Original*

A Minstrel Book published by
POCKET BOOKS, a division of Simon & Schuster Inc.
1230 Avenue of the Americas, New York, NY 10020

ISBN: 0-671-50515-7

First Minstrel Books printing October 1996

10  9  8  7  6  5  4  3  2  1

Cover art by Ted Sizemore

Printed in the U.S.A.

# Contents

# THE MYSTERY AT
# THE CRYSTAL PALACE

# 1

## Ice Folly

"Are we almost there?" Bess Marvin asked. Her teeth were chattering. "I feel like a giant Popsicle."

"Don't you ever think of anything that's not related to food?" her cousin, George Fayne, said. George loved to tease Bess about her love for sweet things.

Nancy Drew tucked her reddish blond hair behind her ears as another gust of wind swept off the Mississippi River. It blasted her face with flying bits of snow that had accumulated from an earlier storm. She nodded toward a glass building at the end of the block. "That must be it."

George squinted at the sign on top of the domed building. The dome was surrounded by tall spires and tapering towers that made it look like a

1

magical castle. "This is it—the Crystal Palace," George said.

The three girls walked briskly to the ice arena, passing a number of restaurants and colorful boutiques. Nancy looked up at the decorative, turret-like columns gleaming in the sunlight under a light dusting of snow.

"The Crystal Palace is *huge*," Bess observed. "Alison must feel like a princess owning this. I half expect some little gnomes to run out to greet us any minute."

"I can't believe Alison inherited this whole arena from her uncle Henry," George said.

Nancy smiled. "And to think she used to play go fish with me."

Alison MacDonald was an old family friend of the Drews, and as a teenager she sometimes baby-sat for Nancy. Nancy still remembered the stories Alison would tell about the summers she spent in Minneapolis with her uncle Henry. Now Nancy understood why Alison had said the Crystal Palace looked like a fairy-tale castle.

"Alison always did love skating," Nancy said.

"When was the last time you saw her, Nan?" Bess asked.

"Not since she left home to go to college," Nancy replied. "I guess it's been six or seven years. After her parents died, Alison didn't have any family left in River Heights."

"How sad." Bess hugged herself to keep warm as they waited for the traffic light to turn green. "I

2

think it's great that you guys have kept in touch all this time. I bet Alison's especially glad now that she needs a good detective."

"I just hope I can help. From what Dad told me, finding Henry MacDonald's missing money is going to be pretty tough," Nancy said.

"So your dad didn't have any ideas at all?" George asked.

Nancy shook her head. In his will Alison's uncle had left his niece a large sum of money in addition to the Crystal Palace. But after he died, Henry MacDonald's lawyers could locate only some of the funds. Alison immediately contacted Nancy's father, a respected attorney in River Heights. Carson Drew was equally puzzled about the money's whereabouts, and since he was wrapped up in a long court case, he couldn't go to Minneapolis for several more weeks. He'd suggested that Alison ask Nancy to look for her uncle's lost money. Nancy had investigated many cases with her father, and on her own, too. She was glad she could use her experience to help her friend.

"Alison and I have both been so busy, I only got to talk to her for a few minutes," Nancy said as the girls dashed across the street. "Dad filled me in on what he knows, but I still have to get all the details from Alison."

"I'm glad Alison invited all three of us," George said as they climbed the granite steps in front of the Crystal Palace. "I can't wait to see the skating competition."

George yanked open a heavy glass door, and Nancy and Bess filed ahead of her into the crowded lobby. They were greeted by a blast of cool, moist air.

Nancy's blue eyes scanned the expansive lobby. The area near the entrance was carpeted and furnished with carved tables and high-back chairs, in keeping with the arena's castle theme. But the mouthwatering aroma of cheeseburgers also hung in the air. Across from the skate rental area, Nancy spotted a snack bar. Sturdy rows of bleachers lined the walls around two full-size ice rinks.

Nancy nodded toward a blond woman who stood near the barrier to the ice. "You're the sports expert, George. Is that Meg Abbott?"

George's dark eyes widened. "The Olympic silver medalist?"

"The one who did those juice commercials on TV?" Bess asked.

"The one and only," a voice said behind Nancy. Nancy whirled around and saw a small, pretty brunette in her midtwenties grinning at her.

"Alison!" Nancy exclaimed, and gave her a big hug. "Do you remember my friends Bess and George?" she asked.

"Of course." Alison greeted them warmly. Her gaze went from tall, dark-haired George to petite, blond Bess. "You two still don't look remotely like first cousins."

"We know," Bess and George replied in unison.

4

Alison led the group to a table near the snack bar. Bess sat down, discreetly slipped off her fleece-lined boots, and began massaging her toes.

"I hope you didn't freeze walking over here," Alison said, watching Bess. "This is the coldest it's been since I moved to Minneapolis. Usually the weather's pretty similar to River Heights'."

"We were fine. Our hotel's only a few blocks away," Nancy reminded her.

Alison leaned forward in her seat. "How *is* the Excelsior? Are you finding everything all right?"

"All right?" George repeated. "It's incredible. You should see the fitness center."

"And the room service is the best," Bess added. "We ate lunch before we came over."

"Hot chocolate, ladies?" A man in his mid-thirties wearing jeans and a blue Crystal Palace sweatshirt leaned over Bess's shoulder. He lowered a tray toward the girls.

Nancy smiled and said, "Speaking of terrific service . . ."

Alison took a ceramic mug topped with whipped cream and a cinnamon stick and passed it to Nancy. "Thank you, Ted. This was so sweet."

Ted smiled, and a small dimple appeared in his cheek. "Just doing my job." He offered the mugs of hot chocolate around, and each young woman took one.

"Ted Marler's my assistant manager," Alison explained. "He's been at the Crystal Palace for ages. I don't know what I'd do without him." She

5

turned to him and said, "But this does go a little beyond the call of duty, Ted."

Ted set down a plate of pastries. "Nothing but the best for our VIP guests," he said. "Nancy, Bess, and George, I presume?"

Alison nodded and said, "By the way, thanks for recommending the Excelsior Hotel. They love it."

Ted beamed. "I'm glad. Let's hope all the skaters who are staying there during the competition feel the same way." Then his expression grew more serious. "Al, do you think you could stop by my office when you're finished here? I'm having a little problem with one of the sponsors."

Nancy saw her friend's shoulders tense. "Thanks," Alison said. "I'll be there in a few minutes."

As Ted disappeared to the back of the arena, Alison drummed her fingers on the marble tabletop. "I wonder what's wrong now." She sighed. "I can't believe Uncle Henry ever thought I was ready for this. You can't imagine how much work goes into preparing for a major competition."

"I don't blame you for being a little worried," George said sympathetically. "The Midwestern Sectional Championships are a pretty big deal."

Alison rolled her eyes. "Please, don't remind me. I can't believe they're starting in two days."

Nancy leaned forward. "Alison, you seem anxious. I know there's a lot riding on this competition, but is there something else going on here?"

Alison sighed. "Yes. If things don't go perfectly

6

this week, I'm afraid I'm going to run the Crystal Palace out of business."

Bess glanced at the groups of teenagers milling around the lobby. Most came to skate, but some came to hang out with their friends. "Business looks pretty good to me," she said.

"It is for now," Alison agreed. "But if anything goes wrong, I'm in big trouble, because I won't have enough money to fix it."

"What happened to the money you inherited from your uncle?" Nancy asked. "I didn't think *all* of it was missing."

"Oh, it isn't. But before I arrived, Ted had to make emergency repairs to the pipes under both ice rinks. They were necessary but expensive," Alison explained. "My budget's almost wiped out."

Now Nancy understood. No wonder Alison was so anxious to locate her uncle's missing money.

Alison gestured toward the platter of rich desserts Ted had brought with the hot chocolate. "Have something to eat. We can talk about the case after I've given you the grand tour."

Bess reached for a coconut-covered fudge brownie. Then she hesitated and pulled back her hand, taking a small bunch of grapes instead.

George sighed. "Are you on a diet again?"

Bess popped a grape in her mouth and said, "Look at all these skinny skaters." She nodded toward the main rink. "Meg Abbott looks even thinner in real life than she does on TV."

7

"I thought she retired from skating years ago," Nancy commented, hoping to distract Bess from the topic of dieting.

"Is Meg here to watch the competition?" George asked.

"Sort of," Alison replied. "She's a coach now, and a few of her students are skating in the sectionals. The rest of the competitors aren't arriving until tomorrow, but Meg trains all her skaters year-round at the Crystal Palace."

"Do you think Meg would give me her autograph?" Bess asked.

"Well," Alison said uncertainly, "we can try." She motioned for Bess to follow her.

The group walked past a hockey game on the rink nearest the snack bar. "If I remember correctly, you were a terrific hockey goalie as a kid," Alison said to George. "Do you still play?"

George nodded, her eyes on the game. "It's great that you have two rinks here. At home we're always competing with the figure skaters for ice time."

"Well, hockey will be on hold here for a few days, I'm afraid," Alison said. "The competition will keep both rinks busy from dawn till late at night almost every day."

On the other rink a Crystal Palace employee was driving the tractorlike Zamboni machine across the ice, scraping snow and squirting water that would freeze and create a smooth surface. A pretty teenage girl had just glided off the ice. She

8

was about sixteen, with long, dark hair and a slight build. An Ace bandage was wrapped around one knee. She walked over to Meg and spoke intently to her.

"She looks familiar," George said. "Wait—I think I read an article about her in a sports magazine. Her name's Sarah something."

Alison nodded. "Sarah Phillips. She's Meg's prize pupil." Alison pointed out a pair who were just entering the arena with skates slung over their shoulders. "And that's Scott Ogden and Amanda Choi. They skate as a pair. Meg's their coach, too."

Scott was wiry and handsome and looked about eighteen. Stylish Amanda, wearing black leggings and a wraparound skating skirt, stood barely as tall as his shoulders. Her silky black hair was pulled into a French braid.

Amanda stood on her tiptoes and whispered something in Scott's ear. Her delicate laugh rippled across the lobby.

"Scott!" Sarah waved from the other side of the arena, then slipped plastic guards over her skate blades. Nancy saw that she narrowed her eyes at Amanda, who quickly moved away from Scott.

Could it be that Sarah was jealous of Amanda? Nancy wondered. Something was definitely going on.

Just then Sarah rushed into Scott's arms. "I haven't seen you in two whole hours. I've missed you so much!"

Meg broke away from the skaters and hurried over to Alison, who introduced her to Nancy, Bess, and George.

"Hi," Meg said curtly to the three girls, then turned to Alison. "I hate to interrupt your social hour, Alison," she said, "but we have a problem here."

Nancy could see Alison gritting her teeth as she turned to face Meg. "Yes?" she said politely.

"Sarah's scheduled to practice during the freestyle session that's about to start. So are Scott and Amanda." Meg frowned. "I specifically requested a separate practice time for them. You know pairs can't get anything accomplished during a crowded freestyle session. And I certainly can't coach them all at the same time."

"I'm sorry, Meg," Alison began. "I—"

"Don't even bother to explain. I'm sick of your excuses," Meg said. "If you keep running things the way you have been, this competition is going to be a total disaster!"

# 2

## Collision Course

Nancy exchanged an uncomfortable look with Bess and George. Poor Alison!

"I'm sorry you feel this way, Meg," Alison said. "If I could—"

Ted Marler seemed to appear from nowhere and came to stand next to Alison. "Excuse me. Did I hear you say there's a problem with the schedule?"

Alison shot Ted a grateful look. "Meg just told me that Scott and Amanda have been scheduled to practice as a pair during the general freestyle session this afternoon. But Meg arranged for them to have separate ice time. Do you know how this happened?"

"I'm afraid I do," Ted said. "I've been training a new employee, and I let him do the schedule this

11

week. I should have checked Pete's work more carefully."

"It's not *your* fault," Meg said.

"I know it's an inconvenience," Ted continued, "but if you'd like to squeeze in an extra practice session for Scott and Amanda, the ice is free tomorrow at five-thirty A.M."

"Thanks, Ted. Please pencil us in." Meg looked around the rink for Sarah, who was sitting on a bench with Scott. "Sarah!" she called, clapping her hands together. "Let's go."

"I guess I'm not going to ask for her autograph," Bess whispered to Nancy as Meg strode angrily toward the ice.

"Maybe another day," Nancy said. She had to admit that Meg seemed to be a no-nonsense coach, though.

Alison breathed a sigh of relief. "You just saved the day," she told Ted. "I never know the right thing to say to Meg. It's a good thing you do."

"I've known Meg a lot longer than you have." Ted winked at Alison. "Don't let her get to you. You're doing a great job."

"I hope so," Alison murmured. "Do you think I should have a talk with Pete about the scheduling?"

Ted shook his head. "I'll speak with him. I'm sure he just made a simple mistake, planning for the competition and everything. Believe me, it can get pretty complicated." Ted ran a hand through his wavy, light brown hair.

"The schedule is usually Ted's job," Alison explained to the girls. "And he's very good at it."

"You're embarrassing me in front of these lovely young ladies," Ted said lightly. "I'd better get to work. I have a million things to do." With a wave, Ted headed toward the back of the arena, passing several local skaters who were arriving to practice during the general freestyle session.

"I'll see you in your office in a little while," Alison called after him.

"Isn't he handsome?" Bess said as she watched Ted leave. "What a great catch."

"Ted is too old for you, Bess," George said.

"I know," Bess said. "I didn't mean for me. But don't you think he's perfect for Alison?"

Alison looked startled. "Oh, no. Ted's like a big brother to me. I mean, he taught me how to skate when I was a little kid. Anyhow," she added, "he's already taken."

"I didn't see a wedding ring," Bess observed.

"No," Alison said, "but he and Meg have gotten really serious this past year. I think Ted's planning to propose soon."

Bess looked across the arena at Meg, who was squeezing drops into her eyes as she waited for her students to take the ice. "Lucky Meg."

A few minutes later Sarah was practicing triple jumps on her section of the crowded rink under Meg's watchful eye. Beside her, Scott and Amanda did side-by-side double axels, struggling to take off, complete two and a half rotations in the air,

13

and land next to each other at exactly the same time.

"Wow," Bess said. "That looks impossible."

"It's one of the most difficult parts of their program," Alison said. "Not only do they both have to execute the jumps cleanly, but they have to be in perfect unison so they land together."

Just then Amanda's skates slid out from under her and she sat down hard on the ice. "All that and they have to stay on their feet too," Alison joked.

Amanda grinned as Scott bent down and offered her his hand. Nancy noted Sarah's displeased expression as she stole a glance at Scott and his skating partner. She scowled as she dug her toe pick into the ice, and then launched into a dizzying triple toe loop.

"Sarah's really good," George said. "I can't believe she can do that with a sore knee." Sarah came out of the jump and bent to adjust the Ace bandage on her leg.

"Oh, Sarah had minor knee surgery a few months ago," Alison explained. "I think she fell down some stairs. But she's practically a hundred percent now. The bandage gives her a little extra support."

"Is it my imagination, or do Sarah's jumps look backward?" Nancy asked Alison.

"It's not your imagination. Most skaters rotate counterclockwise in the air," Alison said. "Sarah's left-handed, and she jumps clockwise."

As Alison said this, Nancy heard a surprised shout from the rink. She turned her head in time to see Sarah and Amanda collide in midair, then crash onto the ice.

By the time Nancy ran around the rink toward the skaters, Meg and Scott were already kneeling beside Sarah and Amanda.

"Are you okay?" Scott asked Sarah.

Sarah nodded. She was pressing her hand against a gaping cut on her left leg. Blood was visible through her white tights. "This is all your fault," she told Amanda.

Amanda sat up slowly, holding the back of her head. She seemed dazed. "What?"

"You crashed into me on purpose," Sarah said in a steely tone.

Amanda shook her head and winced. "You've got to be kidding. I started my jump first. *You* were supposed to look out for *me.*"

Nancy watched Scott shift his gaze from one skater to the other.

"Nothing would make you happier than if I got hurt so I couldn't skate with Scott," Amanda told Sarah. "Why are you so jealous? You don't have any reason to be."

"I'm not jealous," Sarah scoffed. "And I'm not buying your Little Miss Innocent act, either. I know you made me fall on purpose."

"We've discussed this before, Amanda," Meg said. "Sarah needs extra room to accommodate her jumps. You weren't using your head. Of

15

course," she added with a glance to Alison, "if it weren't for this stupid scheduling error, you two wouldn't have been out on the ice together to begin with."

Alison bit her lip. She motioned to a stocky, sandy-haired man who was passing by. "Pete!"

Nancy recognized him as the Zamboni driver. He must be Pete Bradley, Nancy realized—the new employee who had made the scheduling mistake.

"That's a nasty cut." Pete looked from Sarah's leg to Alison. "What happened?"

"Pete, could you help Meg take Sarah to the first-aid room?" Alison asked quietly. "The trainer should take a look at that leg."

"Sure." Pete and Scott helped Sarah to her feet, and the group hobbled off toward the rear of the arena. The others moved to the edge of the rink.

Amanda drew in a deep breath. For a moment Nancy thought she was going to burst into tears.

Alison squeezed Amanda's hand. "Don't worry, Amanda. Sarah will calm down once she realizes her injury isn't serious."

Amanda looked down at the ice. "You know, skating with Scott is great, but sometimes I wonder if it's worth it. Sarah's so mean to me, and Meg always sticks up for her. Always."

"I don't care what Meg says," George told Amanda. "I know the rules of skating etiquette, and I'm sure the fall was Sarah's fault."

16

Amanda glanced up at George. "Thanks. That makes me feel better."

"We've been watching you skate with Scott," Bess added. "You guys are really good."

"I wouldn't say 'really good.' We haven't been together long enough." Amanda smiled shyly. "But we're getting there. When I left my old coach to skate with Scott, I promised myself we would make it to nationals within two years."

"The top three finishers at sectionals go on to the national championships, right?" George asked.

Alison nodded, turning to Amanda. "I didn't realize you switched coaches so you could skate with Scott. I thought you left Joe Vesella because you weren't happy with him."

"I wasn't unhappy. It's just that with Mr. Vesella I was always second-best to the great Kerri Welch." Amanda rolled her eyes.

"Kerri Welch?" Nancy repeated. "Wasn't she a national figure-skating champion?"

Amanda nodded. "Two years ago. But she sat out last season with ankle injuries, and I don't think she's in top form. If Sarah performs well, she can probably beat Kerri this year." Amanda shook her head. "Well, I can't worry about Sarah and Kerri. I should go back on the ice and get to work."

"That's the attitude." Alison patted her on the shoulder.

Amanda returned to the rink and warmed up with some easy spins and jumps. "What a tough situation for her," George said. "I wouldn't want to spend every day training with a jealous skater's boyfriend."

"Me, neither," Alison said. "I think Amanda's handling it well, though."

"I'm surprised Scott and Sarah don't skate together as a pair," Bess remarked.

"They used to," Alison said. "They were one of the best pairs in the country until Sarah decided she wanted to concentrate on her singles skating. That's when Meg thought of teaming Scott with Amanda."

"It seems to me that matching compatible skaters would be hard," Nancy said.

Alison nodded. "It sure is. There are a lot of factors to think about—age, skating style, height . . . And skating with a partner is a big change from skating by yourself. Not many people can do it well. Considering their short time together, Scott and Amanda are amazingly good. Meg really lucked out."

"It can't be all luck," George commented. "I mean, Meg has to be a pretty decent coach if all her skaters are doing so well, right?"

"Oh, she is," Alison said. "She's a wonderful coach. Although her interpersonal skills could use some work," she added dryly.

"And she always seemed so nice on TV," Bess said.

Alison shrugged. "Uncle Henry loved working with Meg. They were great friends. But since Uncle Henry died and I took over the Crystal Palace, she's been impossible."

"And you have no idea why?" Nancy asked.

"I know Meg's had some financial problems lately," Alison said. "She's stopped getting offers to do commercials, and she doesn't skate in professional exhibitions anymore. I think she resents me because I inherited so much money from Uncle Henry."

Nancy digested this information. If Meg had been close to Henry MacDonald, perhaps he had discussed his financial affairs with her. And if Meg was desperate for cash, Nancy thought, maybe she was the wrong person for Henry to confide in.

"Do you think Meg might know anything about your uncle's missing money?" Nancy asked Alison.

Alison shook her head firmly. "Uncle Henry was so secretive. He never discussed his finances with anyone. He didn't even trust his own accountants." She smiled ruefully. "If he had, we wouldn't be in this predicament."

"Uncle Henry may have been cautious," Nancy pointed out, "but he did trust you, Alison. You were his only living relative. Why didn't he leave you some sort of clue to what he did with the rest of his money? After all, it's rightfully yours now."

Alison looked Nancy in the eye and said, "That's a good question. Uncle Henry's lawyers think the money was probably stolen. Do you agree?"

"It's a possibility," Nancy acknowledged. "It's also possible he invested the funds."

"That makes the most sense to me," Alison said. "Uncle Henry loved to play the commodities market. That's how he made his fortune."

Nancy nodded. "That's what my dad said. But we can't figure out why nobody's found any written record if your uncle made some type of investment. I understand he kept detailed files."

Alison sighed. "He did. That's why this doesn't make any sense. I have drawers and drawers full of his personal papers in my office. He documented every penny he ever spent."

"Which is probably how he stayed so rich," Bess said.

Alison smiled. "I'm sure you're right, Bess. Uncle Henry wasn't stingy, but he was careful with his money. He installed a security system at the house that's practically foolproof, but he still felt safer hiding his valuables. He stashed them in some pretty strange places, too, if you ask me."

Nancy's ears perked up. "Really? Like where?"

"Well . . ." Alison smiled and got a wistful look in her eyes. "One summer when I was little, I was having cereal for breakfast. I thought I found one of those toy prizes in my bowl. It turned out to be Uncle Henry's antique pocket watch. He'd hidden it in the cereal box and forgotten about it." Alison laughed. "I *thought* those Frosted Crispies tasted awfully stale."

George saw Nancy's pensive look and asked, "What is it, Nan?"

"I was just thinking . . ." Nancy said slowly. "If your uncle had a habit of stashing things in weird places, Alison, maybe he hid the money you inherited."

"I sure hope you're right. But unless he buried it in the backyard, it's not at the house he lived in," Alison said. "I've been living there for two months, and I've looked everywhere. Besides, I know all his secret hiding places."

"It would be great if we could learn a little more about your uncle's interests and hobbies," Nancy said. "And I'd like to look through his financial records. My dad said he didn't have a chance to examine all of them. I'm sure your uncle's lawyers didn't miss anything, but it's worth another try."

Alison nodded. "I got everything together for you this morning. Come on. I'll show you my office."

"Alison." It was Sarah. She limped slightly as she approached the group.

Alison glanced down at Sarah's bandaged leg. "Hi. How's the cut?"

"It's okay," Sarah said. "I don't need stitches."

"I'm so glad." Alison introduced Sarah to Nancy, Bess, and George.

Sarah shook their hands graciously. "I don't

21

mean to interrupt, but are you going back to your office?" she asked Alison. "It's locked, and I'd like to pick up my tape."

Alison looked confused. "Tape?"

"The videotape I made of my practice session," Sarah said. "Remember, I was watching it on your VCR? My triple lutz needs to be perfect if I'm going to beat Kerri Welch this week."

"You're taping your practice sessions?" George asked.

"It was Alison's uncle's idea," Sarah said. "He always had a video camera at the rink. He would tape our sessions so we could watch them later and see our mistakes."

"What a great teaching technique," George said.

Sarah nodded. "It works, too. I tape at least one practice a week."

"I'm glad you've found it helpful," Alison said. She led the group to the office area at the rear of the arena.

Bess's blue eyes grew wide when she saw Alison's spacious office. She examined the plush carpeting and ran her hand over the mauve textured wallpaper. "Did your uncle Henry decorate this office?"

Alison's hazel eyes twinkled. "Yes, but I *did* add a few personal touches."

"I love those Olympics prints on that wall," George said. The rest of the office was adorned with reproductions of famous paintings of winter scenes. Nancy glanced at them and then at the two-foot-high stack of paper on Alison's desk. Uncle Henry's records, she guessed.

Bess spotted a large crystal figure on Alison's desk and touched it gingerly. It was a delicate sculpture of a skater poised on a thick circle of frosted glass that looked just like ice. "This is beautiful!" she exclaimed. "Where did you get it?"

"A long time ago, I bought Uncle Henry an ice sculpture very similar to this at the St. Paul Winter Carnival," Alison explained. She turned the sculpture around and admired it from a different angle. "We used to go every year. I wish you could all be here for the carnival. It's so much fun."

"It really is," Sarah chimed in. "Scott and Amanda—" She abruptly stopped speaking, then went on. "Scott and I are going. I'm skating an exhibition this year."

"That's great," Nancy said. "It does sound like fun."

Bess turned to Alison. "So you bought your uncle an ice sculpture. This obviously isn't it."

"Oh, no. Of course, the ice sculpture melted. But Uncle Henry liked it so much, he took a photo of it, then commissioned an artist friend of his to make this statue." Alison smiled, her eyes filling with tears. "He said he would look at it whenever he missed me and feel that I wasn't so far away, after all."

Nancy put a comforting hand on her friend's

23

shoulder. Alison cleared her throat and said, "I'm sorry. I didn't mean to get so emotional." Businesslike, she turned to a large oak filing cabinet in the corner. "Here's a good place for you to start, Nancy."

Sarah moved over to the credenza, which held a VCR and large-screen television set. "Alison, did you remove my tape?" she asked. "I left it in the VCR."

Alison frowned. "No, I didn't. Isn't it there?"

"No," Sarah replied, her voice frantic. "Somebody stole it!"

# 3

## A Message in the Mirror

"Sarah," Alison said calmly, "I was alone in my office most of the afternoon, and I locked the door when I left. I'm sure your tape is here. You must have taken it out of the VCR and put it down somewhere."

"Maybe it fell behind the credenza," Bess said. She and George pulled the credenza away from the wall, but they found only a penny and a bent paper clip.

Nancy and Sarah looked under the file folders on Alison's desk. There was no sign of the tape.

"I'm sorry, Sarah," Alison said. "I don't know what to tell you. I guess you'll just have to make another tape."

"You don't understand!" Sarah exclaimed, her voice rising in desperation. "I *have* to find this one."

25

"Why?" Nancy asked her. "What's so special about this particular tape?" And why would Sarah think someone might want to steal it? Nancy thought privately.

"Never mind," Sarah blurted out, hurrying toward the door. "Just promise you won't tell Meg anything about this, okay?"

Alison exchanged a bewildered look with Nancy as Sarah rushed out.

"That was weird," George said.

Alison shrugged. "Oh, well. Sarah's a little scattered sometimes. I'm sure she just misplaced her tape. Anyhow, I don't have time to worry about it now. It's going to be a zoo tomorrow with all the competitors arriving to practice on the ice. And Kerri Welch will be here, too, which means the press might show up. I hope everything goes okay." She sighed. "That reminds me, I have to talk to Ted about the sponsor problem. . . ."

"We know you're busy," Nancy said quickly. "I'll just grab some files and we'll get out of your hair, okay?"

Alison looked grateful. "You're sure you don't mind?"

"Of course not." Nancy took half the stack of paperwork from Alison's desk, and George took the other half. "We've got plenty of things to keep us busy."

"Don't work too hard," Alison said. She handed Nancy and George tote bags for the papers. "I want you to see the sights while you're here in the Twin Cities."

"I read in my guide book that the Walker Art Center is supposed to be fantastic," Bess said.

"It is," Alison agreed. "There's an incredible outdoor sculpture garden. And if you want to learn more about Uncle Henry's hobbies, he was one of the museum's patrons. He used to take me there all the time. Trust me, you'll love it."

Nancy turned to Bess and George. "Shall we?"

"Sure you won't turn into a giant Popsicle if we go to an outdoor sculpture garden?" George asked Bess.

Bess sighed dramatically. "I think I can brave the elements for the sake of great art."

"Make sure you see Uncle Henry's favorite sculpture," Alison told them. *The Six Crystals.*"

Nancy grinned. "We won't miss it," she said.

Pete was walking past Alison's office as Nancy, Bess, and George entered the hallway. "Those bags look heavy. Do you need some help?" he asked them.

"Thanks, but we're okay," Nancy said.

"Working already, I see." Pete shook his head. "Alison said you were a dedicated detective, Nancy, but I thought you'd at least take a day to explore Minneapolis."

"We're going to the Walker Art Center," Bess said, "as soon as we drop off Uncle Henry's files at our hotel."

Pete smiled. "You'll have a great time at the Walker. And if you don't mind a little advice, as a native Minnesotan, I would suggest you start in the sculpture garden."

"Why?" George asked.

"As the sun goes down, so does the temperature. You don't want to be outdoors for long once that happens. Trust me."

Nancy laughed as Bess nodded vigorously and said, "Thank you. That sounds like good advice."

Half an hour later Bess paused in front of a frozen pond in the sculpture garden. She pulled a wayward strand of hair from her face while George stepped back to admire the huge sculpture above the reflecting pond.

"Is this a spoon?" George asked Nancy in awe.

Nancy looked at her museum brochure as they continued down the walkway. "It's called *Spoonbridge and Cherry*. The spoon is fifty-two feet long, and the cherry weighs twelve hundred pounds. That would make quite an ice-cream sundae."

"Yum. That sounds really good right now." Bess shivered. "Or it would if I weren't so cold. Oh, look! There's *The Six Crystals*." She squinted at the sculpture. "Is it a bench?"

"A sculpture and a bench, all in one. The brochure says you can sit on it." Nancy started after Bess as she moved toward the five-piece granite and cast-iron sculpture built on a slab of concrete. Nancy could see where it got its name. The geometric design did remind her of crystals.

"Pretty fancy bench," Bess said.

Nancy had the creepy feeling that someone was watching her. She spun around, but the only person she saw was Ted Marler. Crouched down on the walkway, he was studying the spoon and cherry sculpture. "Hi," Nancy called, walking back toward him.

Ted looked surprised to see her. He stood up and brushed off the knees of his jeans. "Hi, yourself. Are you and your friends sightseeing before you get busy on your case?"

Nancy nodded. "I'm surprised *you* have time to do anything but work this week."

"Me, too." Ted smiled. "Alison and I cleared up our sponsor problem, so Meg and I decided to steal an afternoon together. I'm sure it'll be our last chance until the competition's over."

Nancy looked around. "Meg's here, too?"

"I was supposed to meet her a few minutes ago. I guess she's running a little late." Ted nodded over his shoulder toward the sculpture. "Isn't this incredible? I can't believe I've lived in Minnesota my whole life and I've never been here before. I should have listened to Alison's uncle when he told me to come."

Bess and George were beckoning to Nancy from their seat on *The Six Crystals*. "Alison said that piece over there was his favorite sculpture," she told Ted. "Would you like to see it? It's called *The Six Crystals.*"

"*The Six Crystals,*" Ted repeated. "Sure."

"I know why Uncle Henry liked this sculpture so much." Bess scooted over to make room on the bench for Nancy as Ted walked around the sculpture, taking it in from all angles. "It's just like the Crystal Palace. A practical work of art." Bess smiled at Ted. "Don't you think so, Ted?"

Ted looked up from his brochure. "I'm sorry. What did you say?"

Nancy saw his preoccupied look. "Is something the matter?"

"No." Ted glanced at his watch. "I was just wondering what's keeping Meg."

George pointed across the garden. "You can ask her yourself. She's right over there."

Ted smiled. "Good eyes, George. Thanks. It was nice seeing you guys." He hurried down the walkway to meet Meg.

Bess shivered. "This has been fun, but I'm getting frostbite. Do you think we can go *inside* the museum now?"

"Gladly," Nancy said.

They walked over a granite crosswalk and entered the Walker Art Center. There they stood in a long line to see the Impressionist paintings of the well-known French artist Claude Monet. The exhibit was on loan from a museum in Boston.

30

Nancy was amazed by the soothing effect of the muted purples, golds, and greens. They were blurred together with broad brush strokes, yet still recognizable as distinct flowers, leaves, and shadows across still waters.

"That was worth the wait," George declared when they returned to the main hallway.

Nancy and Bess nodded. "Now where?" Bess asked as Nancy studied her brochure.

"There's a film presentation on the Amazon. Or—"

Bess tapped Nancy's shoulder. "Look. There's Ted again."

Nancy followed Bess's gaze to see Ted talking with a gray-haired man in a business suit.

". . . I'm sorry I couldn't be of more help," the man was saying. "But as I said, a Noguchi is always a good investment. If you're thinking seriously about making a purchase for Meg . . ."

Ted looked up and noticed Nancy and her friends. "Hello again." He turned to the man. "Edward Neville, Walker curator, meet Nancy Drew, Bess Marvin, and George Fayne. They're visiting Alison."

Mr. Neville shook their hands. "Pleased to meet you. Are you enjoying your visit?"

"Oh, yes. Very much, thank you, Mr. Neville," Nancy replied. "We're just on our way to the Amazon film right now. Pardon us, but we don't want to be late."

31

Bess and George followed Nancy as she hurried around the corner and stopped. She strained to hear Ted's conversation, but he and Mr. Neville moved out of earshot.

"When did we decide to go to the Amazon presentation?" Bess asked.

"We didn't," Nancy replied. "Did you hear what Ted and the curator were talking about?"

George nodded. "I think Ted wants to buy a piece of artwork for Meg."

"How incredibly sweet," Bess said.

"How incredibly expensive," Nancy said. "The curator mentioned investing in a Noguchi. Well, I saw some of Isamu Noguchi's sculptures in the garden. They've got to be worth a fortune."

Bess furrowed her brow. "Is Ted rich? How much money can he make as Alison's assistant manager?"

"Not *that* much," George said.

"Exactly. And if Ted didn't make the money at his job, where did he get it?"

"You're thinking he might know something about Uncle Henry's missing money." Bess frowned and said, "He seems too nice to be a thief."

"I hope I'm wrong," Nancy said. "I like Ted, too."

"So does Alison," Bess reminded her.

On the way back to the hotel, Nancy debated whether she should confide her suspicions to Alison. She might be able to provide helpful information about Ted's background. On the other hand, Alison trusted Ted. If she knew he might be the thief, she would probably treat him differently, and that could blow their investigation. Nancy decided to remain silent for now.

"Dibs on the bathroom!" Bess called, rummaging through her purse as Nancy unlocked the door to their hotel room. Bess gripped her hairbrush in one hand and a scrunchie in the other, prepared to do battle with the tangled mass of hair that the wind had created.

As Bess barged ahead of her into the room, Nancy flicked on the lights. The door to the room adjoining theirs was open. That's strange, Nancy thought. She was pretty sure it had been locked when they left.

From the bathroom, Bess uttered a small shriek.

George chuckled. "Your hair doesn't look *that* bad, Bess."

Bess threw open the bathroom door, her face ashen. "I think you guys had better come in here."

A chill ran through Nancy when she saw what had frightened Bess. While they were gone, someone had scrawled a message across the mirror in bold crimson letters: "Roses are red, violets are blue, soon you'll be dead, dear Nancy Drew."

"Well, that's short and to the point," Nancy said after a moment. She noted the peculiar slant of the handwriting, which was common in left-handed people. Sarah Phillips was left-handed, she thought, but so was ten percent of the population.

"Is it blood?" Bess stammered, stepping back from the sink.

Her heart pounding, Nancy willed herself to stay calm. "No, it's only lipstick," she said.

"Oh, you're right," Bess said. "Whew! That's a relief." She examined the lipstick on the mirror more closely. "You know, I could be wrong, but I think . . ." She rummaged through a plastic make-up pouch next to the sink and pulled out a tube of lipstick. "It looks like the same shade I wear—Fire and Ice. Look."

Bess drew a line down the mirror with her lipstick. Nancy nodded. It was a perfect match.

"Fire and Ice," George said. "How appropriate."

Nancy gently pulled Bess's hand away from the mirror. "Don't touch it until I call hotel security, okay? I'll check and see whether anything's been stolen."

"Come on, Bess," George said as soon as they went through their belongings and saw that nothing valuable was missing. "Let's scope out the restaurants downstairs and decide where to have dinner."

"How can you think about food at a time like this?" Bess asked indignantly.

George grinned. "I guess I've spent too much time around you."

"What is that supposed to mean?" Bess demanded, following George into the hallway.

Although none of their belongings was missing, Nancy saw that some of Uncle Henry's files had been removed from one of the tote bags. She hoped that Alison could tell her which ones were gone. It could have been information crucial to the case.

The Excelsior's security chief arrived a few minutes later. He introduced himself as Mr. Washington. "I promise you we'll get to the bottom of this, Ms. Drew. And I never tell a lie," he added with a smile. But as soon as he saw the sinister message written on the mirror, his expression grew serious. "It seems this was no ordinary break-in. Would you care to fill me in?"

Without giving away too many details, Nancy explained that she was a private detective working on a case at the Crystal Palace.

"And you think this incident is related to your case?" Mr. Washington asked.

Nancy nodded. Mr. Washington knelt on the rug and examined the lock on the room's outer door. "This lock is in perfect working order."

Nancy nodded. She knew the key card system the hotel used was practically tamper-proof. She was also sure the magnetic lock hadn't been picked. Either the intruder had gotten hold of the key card or he or she had entered through the room next door. The door to the adjoining room had been open when Nancy walked in, but it could have been used as an escape route.

"I'll check with the maids," Mr. Washington said. "One of their master keys may have been misplaced—although I should have been told, if that's the case," he added sternly. "I'll also speak with Mr. Russo, the hotel guest next door, as soon as he gets in."

Nancy thanked Mr. Washington.

"I'll give you a progress report as soon as I have some answers," he promised. He left, and Nancy locked the door behind him.

Now more than ever, Nancy was determined to solve this mystery. Someone was trying to scare her off the case. That must mean she was on the right track. She couldn't wait to take a good look at Uncle Henry's files. She could think of only one reason they had been disturbed during the break-in. The intruder must have thought they contained information about the missing money.

Nancy heard a key card being inserted in the door. A moment later George called out, "We're back." She and Bess came into the room.

"It's total chaos downstairs," George said. "Skaters and luggage everywhere. So what's going on?"

"The intruder definitely went through these files." Nancy lifted a stack of folders and carried it over to the bed. "I want to know why."

"Okay. But you can take a dinner break first, can't you?" George asked.

Nancy lifted a menu from the nightstand. "Why don't we order room service?"

Bess grabbed the menu away from Nancy. "We already made reservations for three at the Chinese restaurant downstairs. It's supposed to be out of this world."

Nancy hesitated. "Well . . ."

"If you come to dinner with us, we'll help you with the files all evening," George offered. "Deal?"

"You guys drive a hard bargain. Deal," Nancy agreed with a laugh. "*If* you'll wait for me to phone Alison and put these files in the hotel safe," she added. "Now that I know somebody's after them, I'm not taking any more chances."

"I think we can live with that," George said.

"I have to admit, that kung pao chicken was worth an hour's delay in the investigation," Nancy told Bess and George when they returned to the room after a delicious dinner.

"I couldn't even tell my vegetable stir-fry was low-fat," Bess said. "Now if only my fortune would come true. . . ." Bess reread the tiny slip of paper from her fortune cookie. " 'You will live in the lap of luxury.' "

"How about a lap full of file folders," George said, plopping a stack on Bess's knees as she made room for herself on the bed. She flicked on the TV and found a basketball game in progress.

After three hours Nancy's eyes were beginning

to cross. Still, she hadn't found any information that seemed useful. "Any luck?" she asked Bess and George, turning off the TV.

Bess yawned. "Nope. I don't even know what I'm looking for."

"I don't know exactly, either," Nancy said, though she knew it was too soon to be discouraged. "Let's go to sleep. There's still a pile of paper in Alison's office, and I'd like to get an early start in the morning."

"How early?" Bess asked warily.

"The rink opens at five-thirty," Nancy replied.

Bess pulled a pillow over her head. "Forget it. I need my beauty sleep."

"She sure does," George told Nancy with a straight face.

Bess whacked George with the pillow. "That's not funny."

It was dark when Nancy and George stepped into the frigid air the next morning. George did stretching exercises as they walked through the quiet city. "Have a nice run," Nancy called when they reached the Crystal Palace and George jogged off down the street.

As she entered the arena, Nancy passed two women in janitorial uniforms who were on their way out. She smiled at them, glancing around the lobby in surprise. Yesterday the arena had been jammed with people. Today there was no one in sight. It was hard to believe a major competition would be taking place here in one day.

Moving to the main rink, Nancy saw that Amanda was the only skater on the ice. Scott and Meg must be running late, she thought. As she passed through the lobby on the way to Alison's office, Nancy watched Amanda practice her double axel while classical music played softly.

Suddenly the music stopped, and the Crystal Palace was plunged into darkness.

Nancy heard Amanda gasp. Then the roar of a motor filled the arena. Lights shone across the rink, capturing Amanda in their blinding beams. Amanda screamed.

Nancy couldn't believe her eyes. The huge Zamboni was bearing down on Amanda. The distance between the skater and the machine quickly decreased, but Amanda didn't move an inch. The glaring lights had caught her frozen in terror!

# 4

## A Golden Clue

Amanda stood rooted in place as the Zamboni roared toward her. Nancy jumped onto the ice, her instincts immediately taking over. She shoved Amanda out of the way and dived to the ice, sliding out from under the Zamboni's heavy wheels. A second later the immense machine rolled over the spot where the girls had just been.

Nancy stood up and extended a hand to Amanda. "Quick. Let's get off the ice."

She heard a crash and spun around. The Zamboni had slammed into the rink's wooden barrier, then ground to a halt. The engine eerily cut off, leaving a silence hanging in the darkness.

"You saved my life." Amanda's voice trembled, but her feet were steady as she led Nancy through the darkness to the edge of the ice.

Nancy groped along the barrier for an opening. "Are you all right?"

"Yes," Amanda whispered. "Are you?"

The arena lights flickered back on. Amanda shielded her eyes as Nancy turned to look at the Zamboni, its front end crumpled against the barrier. The driver was gone.

"Stay here," Nancy told Amanda. She helped her into a chair. Then she hurried over to the abandoned machine and scrutinized the ice. If it was soft enough, she thought, the driver might have left footprints on it when he fled.

Nancy was disappointed to see that the surface was smooth and hard. However, a glint of metal under the Zamboni caught her eye.

Nancy winced as she knelt, her knees tender from the dive onto the ice. She reached under the front tire and carefully fished out a large gold barrette. Turning it over in her hand, she admired the unique lacy design. Sparkling rhinestones were imbedded in the center. Urgent voices made Nancy look up.

"Amanda!" Alison called, running to the rink with Ted on her heels. "What happened?"

Ted exclaimed in dismay when he saw the damaged Zamboni.

"We had a little . . . accident," Nancy explained.

Alison took in Amanda's shredded tights and the bits of ice clinging to Nancy's green angora sweater. "Are you all right?"

41

Amanda nodded shakily.

As Nancy explained what had happened, Alison gasped. "Who would do such a thing?" she said.

Amanda opened her mouth, then closed it again. Nancy wondered what she was thinking. "Do you have any ideas, Amanda?"

Amanda shook her head.

Nancy showed the barrette to Amanda. "I found this near the Zamboni. Is it yours?"

Amanda's eyes grew wide. She shook her head.

Nancy wasn't surprised. The showy barrette didn't seem to fit Amanda's sophisticated, classic style. And if it wasn't Amanda's, Nancy figured it belonged to whoever had driven the Zamboni.

"That's great, Nan," Alison said. "At least you have a clue."

Ted returned from inspecting the Zamboni. "The motor runs, but the snow-dumping mechanism's out of commission," he reported. He smiled at Amanda. "I'm glad you're okay."

"That's the important part," Alison said.

Ted went back to the Zamboni. He climbed in and backed it slowly off the ice.

Nancy pocketed the barrette. "What are you going to do if the Zamboni doesn't work?" she asked Alison.

"Thankfully, we have another one," Alison said. "It's not in the greatest shape, but it'll do the job." She looked at her watch. "It's almost six. Where are Scott and Meg?"

"Meg is right here." Meg strode into the lobby, followed by Scott and Sarah.

"Where have you guys been?" Amanda demanded.

"I overslept," Scott murmured. He exchanged a look with Sarah. Nancy thought she caught a fleeting expression of guilt on his face.

Meg ignored Amanda's question. She took in Amanda's ragged appearance. "Rough practice session?" Meg asked.

When Amanda explained what had happened with the Zamboni, Meg's face turned red. "Haven't you ever heard of security?" she shouted to Alison.

"I'm as upset about this as you are," Alison said. "Could we please discuss this calmly and rationally in my office?"

Meg turned to Amanda. "Do you feel up to skating this morning?"

Amanda nodded.

"All right." Meg motioned toward the ice. "Start working on your lifts," she said to Scott and Amanda. "I'll be back soon."

Meg followed Alison to her office, while Scott and Amanda moved toward the ice. Sarah climbed up into the bleachers to watch.

Nancy stopped Ted as he passed by. "Could I ask you a few questions?" she asked.

Ted's dimple appeared. "Sure. What can I do for you?"

43

Nancy was surprised by his easy manner. If he was nervous that she might question him about Henry MacDonald's missing money, it didn't show. "Who might know how to operate a Zamboni?" Nancy asked.

Ted shrugged. "Just about anybody who's been around an ice rink. It's pretty simple."

"Who usually drives the Zamboni here at the Crystal Palace?"

"Most of the time it's Pete," Ted said. "But he couldn't have been the person who tried to run down Amanda. He was in my office when the lights went out."

Nancy nodded. "Do you know what caused the electricity to fail?"

"Somebody tripped the circuit breaker. I sent Pete to restore power," Ted replied.

"Is the breaker located near the rink?"

Ted nodded, pointing across the room. "It's right over there, around the corner."

"Around the corner," Nancy repeated. "That means our Zamboni driver must have had an accomplice."

Ted cocked his head. "Why do you say that?"

"Because I heard the Zamboni motor start a split second after the lights went out," Nancy said. "There's no way the driver had time to trip the circuit breaker and run over to the Zamboni."

"I guess that makes sense." Ted looked impressed. "Alison was right when she said you're a talented detective. Do you have any more questions for me?"

Nancy shook her head. "Not right now. Thanks."

"Glad to be of service." Ted started to go, then turned back to Nancy. "I sure hope you can help Alison find her uncle's missing money. Alison's a good kid. She doesn't deserve all these hassles."

Six hours later Nancy's head throbbed as she leaned over to pull more files from Alison's cabinet drawer. Hard as she tried, she couldn't seem to concentrate on the missing money. All she could think about was Amanda's encounter with the Zamboni. Who would want to hurt Amanda? Sarah? If so, it would be at the expense of Scott's skating career. After all, he couldn't skate without a partner. Would Sarah do that to her own boyfriend? And who might be her accomplice?

Nancy rubbed her eyes. Her knees were stiff and sore from the fall and from sitting so long. She needed to take a break.

Wandering out to the Crystal Palace lobby, Nancy spotted Bess's bright turquoise beret in the middle of the crowd. She waved and called out, "Bess!"

Bess motioned for Nancy to join her in the bleachers. "I'm having so much fun," she said a few moments later. "How about you?"

Nancy rolled her eyes. "Those files are endless.

But there was an interesting development this morning."

Bess nodded. "Oh, I know. You were nearly mowed down by a Zamboni. I'm so glad you're okay."

Nancy's eyes widened. "You heard about it?"

"Of course." Bess smoothed her leather skirt over her knees. "All the skaters are talking about it."

"You've met the skaters?"

"Pete gave me the complete rundown." Bess pointed out some of the men's seniors. "That's Kyong Oh. And Danny Silver. And see that couple? I thought they were pairs skaters, but they're really ice dancers. They have to do traditional dances like the waltz, but on skates."

Nancy's eyes strayed to the hockey rink, which was now filled with young boys and girls performing amazingly difficult jumps. "What's with all the kids?"

"Aren't they adorable?" Bess grinned. "They're competing in the junior and novice divisions. And see that tiny girl on the main rink?"

Nancy nodded as Bess pointed out a graceful, African-American girl who landed a beautiful triple jump, followed immediately by a double. "That's Dominique Morrow. She's only thirteen, but she's entered the senior competition this year."

Nancy watched as Dominique skated past an

46

older competitor, who had red hair and was wearing a sequined unitard. "I've seen that redhead on television," Nancy said. "Isn't that Kerri Welch?"

Bess waved at Kerri. "Yes. She's nice."

Kerri waved back cheerfully and skated over to where Nancy and Bess were sitting. She skidded to a halt, spraying ice into the air. Bess introduced her to Nancy.

"So this is the famous detective," Kerri said with a friendly smile. Her upturned nose was sprinkled with freckles. "Bess told me all about you."

Nancy blushed in embarrassment and elbowed Bess. "So this is the famous skater. Bess told me all about *you*."

"Kerri's routine is amazing," Bess gushed. "And she makes it look so easy."

"Thanks." Kerri turned to wave at Amanda, who was passing through the lobby. "Amanda Choi's skating has improved about a hundred percent," she remarked. "I hope she and Scott do well in the competition."

Nancy was surprised and somewhat pleased to hear Kerri speak kindly of Amanda. Amanda certainly didn't seem too fond of her. Nancy remembered Amanda saying she had always felt she was second-best when she and Kerri had shared the same coach.

Kerri leaned against the barrier, facing Nancy and Bess. "I heard that somebody tried to kill

47

Amanda with a Zamboni today." She lowered her voice. "What's your opinion, Nancy? Was it Sarah?"

"Well . . ." Nancy tried to think of a diplomatic answer. She was distracted when Meg and Sarah came into the lobby and walked past the bleachers.

"How are you supposed to skate with your hair in your face?" Meg said impatiently. "How many times do I have to tell you to put it up?"

With a sigh Sarah pulled her shimmering dark hair into a ponytail, reached into the pocket of her sweatshirt, and took out a barrette. As she fastened it in her hair, Nancy's eye caught something sparkling. She looked closer and saw that it was rhinestones glinting. The barrette Sarah wore was identical to the one Nancy had found next to the Zamboni.

# 5

## *Dynosour Grapes*

Nancy was glad to find Alison sitting at her desk, going through some paperwork. She was eager to hear what Alison thought about the rivalry between Sarah and Amanda.

Alison's mouth dropped open when Nancy told her about Sarah's barrette. "I can't believe Sarah would try to harm Amanda. At least not that way." Alison shuddered.

"Do you have any idea who might want to hurt her?" Nancy asked. "Another competitor, maybe?" She explained to Alison that she thought the Zamboni driver had had an accomplice.

Alison shook her head slowly. "I don't know anyone who has anything against Amanda. Scott and Amanda are great skaters, but I doubt they'll place in the top three at this competition. And Amanda's well liked by the other skaters—"

49

"Except Sarah," Nancy said.

Alison sighed. "I guess I can't ignore the facts. Sarah must have been the Zamboni driver. There's no other explanation."

"One thing about this bothers me, though. Sarah might dislike Amanda, but she loves Scott," Nancy said. "Why would she jeopardize his skating career by trying to hurt Amanda?"

"You're right," Alison said. "Sarah is Scott's biggest supporter. And he'd never find another partner like Amanda. If something happened to her, his skating career would probably be history. It doesn't make sense."

"That's why I'm not jumping to any conclusions yet," Nancy said.

Alison patted a stack of files in front of her. "So, have you jumped to any conclusions about Uncle Henry's missing money?"

"Afraid not." Nancy moved to the desk and handed Alison a file. "I do have a question, though."

Alison took the folder Nancy handed her and skimmed its contents.

"I was looking through the arena's repair records," Nancy continued, "and I see that your uncle wrote a large check last year to Waterworks, Inc. Most of the file is detailed, but there's no notation explaining what the repairs were," Nancy said.

Alison nodded. "I know. Ted and I were curious about the same thing."

"I tried contacting Waterworks, but they've gone out of business," Nancy said.

"Waterworks was pretty much a one-man operation. The owner, Mr. Peters, had been planning to retire to Florida for as long as I can remember. Well, he finally did it. In fact, he was so anxious to get out of here before winter hit that he had his son take care of closing down the business. Ted and I tried to get in touch with Mr. Peters in Florida, but unfortunately, he didn't leave a forwarding address."

"What about Mr. Peters's son?" Nancy wondered. "Couldn't he help you?"

Alison smiled ruefully. "Hard to believe, but Brad hasn't taken a vacation in ten years, and now he's on a three-month trip to the Caribbean. He works at your hotel, the Excelsior. Ted's going to call him when he gets back."

Nancy decided to seize the opportunity to learn a little more about Ted. "I'm surprised Ted isn't familiar with the repairs your uncle had Waterworks make," she said. "Hasn't he been at the Crystal Palace for a long time?"

"Yes," Alison replied. "But he took a leave of absence for six months last year when his mother died."

Nancy, who had lost her own mother when she was a little girl, immediately felt sympathetic toward Ted. But even this information struck her as odd. "Six months? That's an awfully long time, isn't it?"

51

"Ted was close to his mother," Alison said. "I know she was sick before she died—confined to bed and nearly blind. Uncle Henry said Ted used to read to her every day."

Now Nancy felt worse than ever about suspecting Ted.

"Apparently," Alison continued, "his mother was rich. Ted was the executor of her estate, and it took him a long time to get all her financial matters settled. I know he inherited a lot of money eventually."

Nancy leaned forward in her seat. "Really?"

Alison laughed. "He hides it well, doesn't he? But believe me, Ted is very rich. He wouldn't have to work for the rest of his life if he didn't want to."

"Then why does he?"

"Ted loves it here," Alison said simply. "His mother brought him to the rink for skating lessons when he was three years old. He says the Crystal Palace is like a part of him. He'd never think of quitting."

Nancy sighed with relief. "You don't know how happy this makes me."

Alison looked at Nancy curiously. "Why?"

"I know how much you like Ted," Nancy said, "so I wasn't looking forward to telling you he was a suspect in the disappearance of your uncle's money. Luckily, that's no longer the case."

Alison shook her head and smiled as Nancy recounted her encounter with Ted at the art museum and her suspicions that he may have stolen her uncle's money. "I'm so glad to learn that Ted's independently wealthy," Nancy concluded. "I should have asked you in the first place."

"I should have told you. Ted's so wonderful, it never crossed my mind you might consider him a suspect."

Nancy rolled up her sleeves and pulled a stack of files toward her. "Well, back to square one, I guess."

Alison stood up. "No, you don't. It's one o'clock. Time for you to take a lunch break. I need to finish up some paperwork in here, anyhow."

Nancy realized she was hungry and decided to grab something from the snack bar. As she rounded the corner by Ted's office, she nearly ran into Bess.

"We were just looking for you," Bess said. "Kerri, George, and I are going to lunch. Want to come?"

Nancy's eyes widened. "Kerri Welch?"

"I invited her to come with us, and she said yes. Her afternoon practice doesn't start for a few hours, and she wants to get some fresh air."

"Sounds like fun," Nancy said. "Where are we going?"

"Follow me," Bess said. Nancy did, outside to the rental car. Soon Nancy was driving the group over the Mississippi River to St. Paul, the sprawling state capital on the opposite bank.

"Why are Minneapolis and St. Paul nicknamed the Twin Cities?" Kerri asked Bess.

Bess flipped through the pages of her guide book. "It doesn't say. But it *does* say that O'Malley's makes the best burgers in St. Paul. Which is exactly what Pete told me."

"Wonderful," Kerri said, patting her stomach. "I'm starving."

Nancy pulled into the parking lot of a quaint redbrick pub, and the four girls climbed out of the car.

"Welcome to O'Malley's," a friendly hostess greeted them a few moments later. She led them to a quiet booth by a window overlooking the water.

"I already know what I want," Kerri said as she took a menu. "A cheeseburger, potato salad, and a chocolate shake."

"Some people can eat anything," Bess said, eyeing Kerri's slender figure.

Kerri laughed. "Hardly. This is a rare treat for me."

Bess frowned as she glanced over the menu. "I'll have a turkey sandwich," she decided. "No mayonnaise."

"Are you nervous about the competition?" Nancy asked Kerri a few minutes later as they dug into their meals. She offered Bess a melon cube from her fruit plate.

Kerri nodded. "I'm surprised I have any appetite at all. Especially after what happened to Amanda this morning."

George stabbed a crouton in her chef's salad with her fork. "What happened to Amanda this morning?"

"You didn't hear?" Bess asked, scraping some potato salad away from her sandwich. "She was almost run over by a killer Zamboni. Nancy pushed her out of the way just in time."

"You're kidding," George said.

"Unfortunately not," Nancy replied.

"That's so weird." George looked thoughtful. "When I was jogging this morning, I could have sworn I saw Scott and Amanda skating on Lake Calhoun. I thought it was strange, because I knew they were supposed to be practicing at the Crystal Palace. Well, now I know I must have been seeing things."

Kerri nodded. "Believe me, Meg is obsessive about being in charge. She would never let Scott and Amanda practice if she wasn't around."

"How do you know that?" Bess wondered.

Kerri took a forkful of potato salad. "Meg used to be my coach."

"That's right. Amanda told me that." Nancy turned to Kerri. "If it's not too personal a question—do you mind my asking why you switched coaches?"

Kerri swallowed. "Not at all," she said. "Meg's a good coach, but she would do anything to win.

55

Anything." She raised her dark eyebrows for emphasis. "Sarah Phillips might think that's okay, but *I* do not."

"So do you like your new coach any better?" George asked.

Kerri nodded. "Definitely. Mr. Vesella's wonderful. He's so calm and patient. I still can't believe Amanda left him to go train with Meg."

"Scott and Amanda are skating well," Nancy said.

Kerri nodded. "Which must be the reason Amanda ended up as Zamboni bait. Sarah can't stand to see anybody else have what she wants." Kerri cleared her throat. "You know, now that Sarah's skating singles, I'm her biggest competition. I guess that means I should watch my back, too," she said lightly.

Nancy didn't know how serious Kerri was about considering Sarah a threat, but she decided to file away the information in her memory. Looking at her watch, she said, "I hope you guys don't mind, but we'd better head back to the arena. It's getting late."

Kerri set her napkin on the table. "I'm ready. Mr. Vesella's pretty understanding, but I don't want to push my luck."

When they entered the Crystal Palace a short while later, Kerri stopped at the snack bar. "I'm thirsty. Does anybody else want anything?"

"No, thanks." Bess looked up at the menu.

"Dynosour Juice. Isn't that the brand Meg used to advertise on TV? 'The juice of champions.' "

Ted was behind the counter, fixing the frozen yogurt machine. "Yep. You wouldn't believe how much of that stuff we've sold this week. It's very popular with skaters." He sighed. "So is frozen yogurt. I think this machine just died of exhaustion."

Kerri looked at the bottles of sparkling purple juice lined up on the counter. "I'll have an extra-large, please."

Kerri's eyes grew wide when the waitress handed her an enormous cup of Dynosour Juice. "I may be the new product spokesperson, but I'm never going to be able to drink all this. Want some?" she asked Nancy, Bess, and George.

Nancy and George shook their heads.

"You're the new Dynosour spokesperson?" Bess asked. She reached for a fresh straw and put it into the cup.

Kerri nodded. "My agent finalized the deal yesterday. I'm making my first commercial as soon as the nationals are over."

"That's terrific," Nancy said, and Bess and George nodded. Bess took the cup and sipped from it while Kerri peeled off her sweater and leggings, then sat on a bench and laced up her skates.

"Thanks, Bess." Kerri took one last sip through her straw before she stepped onto the ice. Nancy

57

lingered by the barrier with Bess and George, watching the skaters for a few minutes. On the padded floor near the rink, Amanda and Scott were practicing lifts.

Meg came to stand near Bess, observing Sarah intently. "Arms tight," Meg called to her.

Nancy smiled as she noticed Kerri's effort to steer clear of Sarah's long, flying jumps. Every few minutes Sarah came to the edge of the ice to talk to her coach.

Nancy watched in amazement as Kerri's coach, Joe Vesella, made her practice the camel spin over and over again. With her arms outstretched, Kerri rotated on her left leg while extending her right leg straight behind her so that it was parallel to the ice. "I can't believe that doesn't make her dizzy," Nancy whispered to George as Kerri spun on the ice.

After several seconds Kerri's right leg sagged. She touched a shaky foot to the ice and stopped spinning.

"I guess it *did* make her dizzy," George said.

Slowly Kerri skated toward the edge of the rink. Then she clutched her stomach and fell to her knees, crying out in pain!

# 6

## Fire and Ice

Joe Vesella spoke calmly to Kerri, then scooped her off the ice and carried her through the lobby. Ted and Alison followed briskly behind them, ignoring the gasps and murmurs of the skaters who had seen Kerri collapse. The group filed down a hall and into an office. The door closed behind them, and Nancy, Bess, and George waited nearby. Other skaters and onlookers gathered in the hall.

A few minutes later Alison came out to the hallway. She looked for and spotted Nancy and then wove her way through the crowd. "Jerry, the trainer, thinks Kerri probably has a bad case of food poisoning. Or it might be a stomach virus. She's going to have a thorough exam at the hospital to be on the safe side."

Nancy exchanged a concerned look with Bess and George. "Maybe lunch at O'Malley's wasn't such a good idea."

"Do you think Kerri's going to be able to skate in the competition?" George asked.

Alison frowned. "Women's singles doesn't start till Friday. I hope she'll be okay by then."

Bess fanned herself with a paper napkin. "Is it hot in here?"

"Hot?" Nancy looked at Bess with concern. "You just said you were cold a few minutes ago."

Bess looked around for a chair and sat down heavily.

"Are you feeling all right?" Nancy asked her.

Bess gulped. "Just a little queasy."

"You look terrible, Bess," Alison said. "Could you have food poisoning, too?"

Bess rested her head against the wall. "I hope not."

Ted came out of the first-aid room and closed the door behind him. He looked startled when he saw Bess's pale face. "Are you sick, too?"

"We're afraid so," Alison said. "I wonder if she should ride in the ambulance with Kerri."

Bess shook her head. "No, I'm okay. I'd just like to go back to the hotel and rest."

Nancy and George helped Bess to her feet.

"You can't walk in your condition. Why don't I give you a ride?" Ted offered.

Bess smiled wanly. "Thanks." The three girls followed Ted out to his car.

"Do you need me to help you to your room?" Ted asked a few moments later. He zipped up the Excelsior's driveway in his sports car and lurched to a halt in front of the double doors.

Bess's face had taken on a greenish tinge. "I think I'm carsick," she whispered to Nancy.

"We'll be okay," Nancy told Ted quickly. "Thanks."

Ted nodded. "You might want something to settle your stomach, Bess. Would you like me to swing by the drugstore?"

"Getting out of this car is the only thing that will settle my stomach," Bess murmured.

"I saw a pharmacy on Lake Street when I was jogging this morning," George said. "You're busy, Ted. Nancy and I can go."

"Are you sure?" Ted asked.

Nancy smiled. "You've done more than enough already. Thanks for all your help."

"Don't mention it." Ted tapped his horn lightly as he sped away.

Half an hour later Bess was snuggled under the quilt in her double bed, snoring softly in her sleep. George and Nancy grabbed their parkas and tiptoed out.

Mr. Washington, the hotel's security chief, stopped them in the lobby. "I was just about to call you," he told Nancy.

"Did you get a lead on the break-in?" Nancy asked him eagerly.

"In a manner of speaking." Mr. Washington's

61

forehead creased in a frown. "I interviewed the gentleman staying in the room next to yours. Mr. Russo says that none of his belongings was disturbed. That means you were the only target, Ms. Drew."

"Did you talk to the maids?" Nancy asked.

Mr. Washington nodded. "None of them claims to have missed a passkey."

"So whoever broke into our room probably did gain access through Mr. Russo's room," Nancy said. "The lock on the adjoining door is flimsy. It wouldn't take much skill to pick it."

"I'm afraid that's true," Mr. Washington agreed. "It's much less secure than the door that leads to the hallway. Also, Mr. Russo told me he met with several clients in his room yesterday. I'd say they're our main suspects, wouldn't you?"

George looked impressed. "I think we're finally getting somewhere."

"Do you know who these clients are?" Nancy asked the security chief.

Mr. Washington shook his head. "Mr. Russo refused to provide me with a list of names, and I can't force him. Unless we involve the police, I don't think we have many options."

Nancy nodded. The last thing she wanted to do was call the police and draw attention to Alison's problems at the arena—particularly during the competition. "I don't think it's necessary to report this to the police," she told Mr. Washington.

"After all, nothing was stolen." Nancy decided she would have a little chat with Mr. Russo herself.

Mr. Washington shrugged. "Whatever you say."

"Thanks for your help. We appreciate it," Nancy said.

"Good luck with your case," Mr. Washington called after them as they headed outside.

At the drugstore Nancy and George surveyed a shelf stocked with stomach remedies. "There are so many to choose from," George said uncertainly.

"Maybe we should ask the pharmacist for some advice," Nancy suggested.

They moved out of the aisle as the bell on the door jangled. Nancy looked up and saw Ted entering the store.

"How's Bess?" he asked.

"Sleeping," Nancy replied.

"That's good. I hope she feels better soon. If I'd known Meg was going to ask me to come to the drugstore, I would have insisted on getting Bess's medicine myself," he said.

A woman wearing a white lab coat came out of the back room as Ted approached the pharmacy counter. She gave Ted a friendly smile as he handed her a prescription slip.

"All ready for sectionals?" he asked her.

The pharmacist smiled. "I've bought four rolls of film. I hope I don't embarrass Scott too much."

"That's what mothers are for," Ted said.

Nancy exchanged a glance with George. So the pharmacist was Scott's mother. She noticed that her plastic name tag said Sheila Ogden.

"I'm surprised Meg's out of eyedrops already," Mrs. Ogden said. "I refilled this just a few weeks ago."

Ted shrugged. "I don't know. Meg said she ran out this morning."

Mrs. Ogden went to work filling the prescription Ted had given her. "Can I help you, ladies?" she asked Nancy and George.

Nancy nodded. "Our friend has a mild case of food poisoning, and we were looking for an over-the-counter medicine that might help."

"This should do the trick." Mrs. Ogden tapped her finger on a blue box and said, "Food poisoning seems to be a popular complaint today. Scott told me what happened to Kerri Welch. I hope she'll be able to skate on Friday. I understand it was touch and go for a little while."

George frowned. "I didn't know she was that sick."

Mrs. Ogden handed a white bag to Ted. "Apparently, she took a turn for the worse. Scott said she's a little better now, but they don't know how long she'll be in the hospital."

Nancy turned to George. "Maybe we'd better check on Bess."

They went to the cash register with the remedy Mrs. Ogden had recommended. Ted stood in line behind them with Meg's prescription and a tube of lipstick. "I hate buying women's things," he said, looking embarrassed.

Nancy smiled. Then she saw the label on Meg's lipstick and did a double-take. It was Fire and Ice—the same shade of lipstick used to leave the threatening message on the mirror!

She paid the cashier and left the store with George. Meg *was* late meeting Ted at the art museum yesterday, Nancy thought. And it was at exactly the time someone was breaking into their room. Could Meg be the culprit?

"I wonder how many women wear that color lipstick," George said as they jogged back to their hotel room.

"You saw the label, too?" Nancy asked.

George nodded. "Bess will know the answer to any and all cosmetics questions. We'll ask her as soon as she wakes up."

"I hope she's all right," Nancy said.

Back in their room, Nancy and George were relieved to find that Bess was still sleeping peacefully, her breathing deep and rhythmic.

"Do you remember what Kerri and Bess had for lunch?" Nancy asked. She handed George some of Uncle Henry's papers to look at.

"Kerri had a cheeseburger," George said, "and fries."

"Potato salad," Nancy said, "not fries."

"Oh, right. And Bess had turkey and potato salad."

"Hmm," Nancy said. "Maybe the potato salad was tainted."

When she awoke several hours later, Bess said she was feeling much better. George showed her the blue box of medicine.

Bess shook her head. "Why do you guys look so worried?" She propped herself up with a pillow. "I told you I didn't feel so bad."

"Because Kerri's in the hospital, and she's really sick." George brought Bess a glass of water with the medicine dissolved in it. "Here. Sip this slowly."

Bess shrugged and took a long drink from the glass, which George held for her. "I can't believe Kerri got so sick. I guess I was lucky." She stifled a yawn. "You guys were even luckier—you didn't get sick at all."

"We didn't eat the same thing," Nancy said.

"Neither did Kerri and I," Bess said.

George turned to Bess. "You and Kerri had potato salad. Nancy and I remembered it came with both your meals, but not with ours."

"Potato salad?" Bess gave George a withering look. "Do you know how many grams of fat are in potato salad? I didn't touch mine."

"Now, that *is* strange." The bed creaked slightly as Nancy stood up. "And Kerri got so much sicker than you did. . . . Did you eat or drink anything else today?"

Bess shook her head. "Just a lot of water. Oh, and a sip of Kerri's Dynosour Juice. She said we could have some," she added defensively.

"That's it!" Nancy exclaimed. "You both had the juice right before you got sick. You only had a little, Bess, so you weren't affected as strongly."

Bess looked skeptical. "I never heard of anyone getting food poisoning from fruit juice."

"Me, neither," Nancy said grimly. "I'm afraid Kerri's drink may have been poisoned." She moved to the phone. "Bess, you threw away the cup at the arena, right? Was there any juice left in it?"

Bess nodded.

"Who are you calling?" George asked Nancy.

"I know the janitorial staff cleans the Crystal Palace in the morning. I'm going to call Alison. I hope we can find that cup and leftover juice and have it tested before somebody gets rid of the trash. Luckily it was in a cup with a tight lid."

Alison was horrified when Nancy told her she suspected Kerri had been poisoned. "I'll meet you at the arena in fifteen minutes," Alison said.

Twenty minutes later Nancy blew on her hands as she waited outside the Crystal Palace for Alison to arrive. She glanced sideways at her watch. It was nearly midnight.

"Sorry I'm late," Alison said as she ran up to the door, pulling a key ring from her pocket. "The one day we close the rink at a decent hour, and here

67

we are at midnight. It figures. Wow. It's warm in here," Alison commented as Nancy followed her into the lobby. She turned on the lights.

Both girls gasped at what they saw. The ice on both rinks was melting.

# 7

## *Midnight Escapades*

"The compressor room, quick!" Alison shouted. She dashed away with Nancy on her heels, heading to the back of the arena. Once there, Alison cast an expert glance at the machinery that froze the ice. Then she let out a frustrated sigh.

"What's wrong?" Nancy asked.

Alison shook her head. "Somebody turned off the compressors. Who would do a thing like that?"

"What can I do to help?"

Alison tossed Nancy her keys. "Could you call Ted and Pete at home? Their numbers are in my phone directory. Explain what happened and tell them I need them down here right away."

Nancy nodded and went to Alison's office. After making the calls, she returned to find the compressors humming and Alison wiping her hands on her jeans. "Everything's working again."

They went back out to the rinks. "What are Ted and Pete going to do when they come?" Nancy asked.

"We have to get a clean-up crew in here right away to sop up the excess water and resurface the ice."

Nancy looked dubiously at the slushy surface on both rinks. "Will that help?"

Alison nodded. "Believe it or not, the ice will be as good as new in about an hour. Whew! I'm so glad you called me tonight, Nan. If nobody had come in until morning, the ice would have been beyond help."

"Then what would you have done?" Nancy asked.

"Had a nervous breakdown," Alison replied with a shaky laugh. "It takes two or three days to put on new ice. We would have had to postpone the competition."

"Yikes," Nancy said. "This is serious sabotage."

"I can't believe this happened." Alison took a deep breath. "But all's well that ends well, right?"

Nancy nodded, but she wondered when they would see an end to the crazy things that were happening. They left the room and walked back to the lobby. Nancy heard Pete's and Ted's voices outside. They'd made record time, Nancy thought. Alison hurried over to the front door to let them in.

Glancing around the lobby, Nancy realized she'd nearly forgotten her reason for coming to the arena at this late hour. She'd meant to retrieve Kerri's drink from the garbage.

She went over to the trash receptacle next to the snack bar, where Bess said she had disposed of the juice. Nancy wondered how many cups would have Dynosour Juice in them. Dozens of other paper cups must have been thrown out during the long day. How would she find Kerri's? Nancy peered inside. That was the least of her worries. The trash bin was empty.

Nancy stopped at each of the other four receptacles in the lobby. All were heaped with candy wrappers, napkins, and cups.

Alison strode over to Nancy. "I see you're on trash patrol. Did you find Kerri's juice?"

Nancy shook her head, trying to remember who was standing near them when Kerri and Bess had been poisoned. Meg, Sarah, Amanda, Scott . . . probably half the skaters in the competition. "Somebody must have watched Bess throw the cup away, then ditched the evidence. Which leads me to believe it *was* evidence," Nancy said.

"Meaning Kerri was poisoned, and the poisoner didn't want you to be able to prove it," Alison concluded.

Nancy nodded. "Do you have a Dumpster out back?"

"Yes," Alison said. "Why?"

"When is it usually emptied?" Nancy asked.

"Early in the morning," Alison answered. Then she peered into Nancy's eyes and said, "You're *not* going to go combing through the trash!" Alison wrinkled her nose. "Anyone careful enough to dispose of the evidence probably took it miles from here."

"She's right, Nancy," Pete said, grimacing as he walked past and overheard the last part of their conversation. "That Dumpster is disgusting. You don't want to go near it."

"I don't *want* to," Nancy said with a sigh. "But I should check, just to be sure."

Pete rolled his eyes. "Now, *that's* dedication."

Out back Alison held a flashlight as Nancy donned an extra-large Crystal Palace sweatshirt and climbed up on a step stool. From there she could see down into the Dumpster. She lifted a large cardboard carton and peered underneath. "There are a lot of boxes in here."

"I know." Alison followed Nancy with the flashlight beam. "Pete's office was completely bare. He didn't seem to care, but it was driving me nuts. Uncle Henry had some old paintings in the attic, so I brought them in to cover Pete's walls. These are the boxes they were in."

"That was thoughtful of you," Nancy said.

Alison shrugged. "They were just prints. Pretty, but not worth anything."

"Did your uncle own any valuable art?" Nancy asked, remembering Henry MacDonald's keen interest in the Walker Art Center. If Alison's uncle was an art collector, maybe he'd invested in an expensive painting or sculpture, she thought. This might give Nancy some new leads to pursue in her search for the missing money.

Alison shook her head. "Uncle Henry thought artwork was a bad investment—too easy to steal. And if it was locked up in a safe somewhere, he couldn't enjoy it."

"Hey, what's this?" Nancy asked suddenly. She picked up a black plastic object.

Alison stood on her tiptoes. "What?"

Nancy brushed off the object. "A videotape." She gave it to Alison, who took it gingerly between two gloved fingers. "It's not marked. I wonder why anyone would throw it away?"

"Well, we can pop it in my VCR and see what it is," Alison said. "Come on. You're not going to find Kerri's drink in there."

"No," Nancy agreed reluctantly. "I guess I'm not."

Back inside the office Alison rewound the tape as Nancy washed up in her bathroom. "Come look at this, Nan!" she called.

Nancy hurried into the office area, drying her hands with a paper towel. She saw Sarah on the TV screen, practicing the same jump over and over again.

"Sarah's missing tape!" Nancy exclaimed.

"It has to be," Alison said. "I know this footage was shot recently, because Sarah just finished making herself that skating outfit a few weeks

73

ago." She looked at Nancy. "Sarah might be a little flighty, but I'm sure she didn't throw away her own tape."

"Anyhow, Sarah was looking for it yesterday," Nancy said. "This tape couldn't have been thrown away until after the Dumpster was emptied this morning."

As the picture became snowy, then went black, Alison took her finger off the Fast-forward button and pressed Rewind. "But why would anybody take it? Sarah could just make another tape if she wanted to. Besides, this one disappeared before any of Sarah's competitors arrived at the arena."

Nancy snapped her fingers. "Wait a minute. Didn't you say your office was locked? If that tape was stolen, somebody must have broken in."

Alison looked startled. "You're right. Ted and I have the only keys."

Nancy knelt down in the corridor to examine the lock on Alison's office door. "There's no sign of forced entry, but sometimes it's practically impossible to tell. . . ." Nancy broke off as she glimpsed a small silver object out of the corner of her eye.

She picked up a tiny screwdriver and rolled it across her palm. "This would make a great lock-pick tool for this type of lock," she said.

Alison examined the screwdriver. "All the skaters carry screwdrivers like this. They use them to tighten their skate blades." Alison closed her eyes in thought. "Hmm . . ."

74

Nancy looked at her intently. "What?"

"I just remembered Meg was yelling at Amanda this morning. Not that that's anything new, but she was upset because Amanda's skate blades were loose. Amanda's usually very conscientious about things like that. Do you think she didn't tighten her blades because she'd lost her screwdriver?" Alison lowered her voice. "Do you think she used it to break into my office to steal Sarah's tape?"

Nancy sighed. "Well, we know Amanda and Sarah don't get along. But why in the world would Amanda go to so much trouble to take Sarah's tape? Why would anyone? They could see Sarah skating anytime. Then again, Sarah *was* awfully upset to find it missing. Not that we have a clue why."

"Why? Why? Why?" Alison said. "My head is spinning."

Nancy nodded ruefully. This case was getting more complicated by the minute.

An hour later Ted's crew had finished resurfacing the ice, and Alison dropped off Nancy at her hotel.

"You've been picking through garbage?" Bess grimaced when Nancy recounted the night's events. "Ugh! I'm glad I had a good excuse to stay home."

"Still feeling okay?" Nancy asked.

Bess nodded. "I guess you didn't find the cup."

Nancy shook her head. "The only things I found

75

were more questions. Not only do we have our original mystery of the missing money, plus the poisonings and death threat . . . now there's theft and sabotage, too."

"And near-death by Zamboni," George added.

"It's weird," Bess commented. "We think Sarah's behind the Zamboni thing, right? Amanda probably stole Sarah's tape. And any of the skaters could have poisoned Kerri to knock her out of the competition. But why would somebody try to melt the ice?"

"If the ice had melted, the competition would have been postponed, right?" George asked.

Nancy nodded.

"I can think of only one person who would want that to happen," George said. "Kerri Welch."

Bess gave George an exasperated look. "Give me a break. Kerri couldn't have turned off the compressors from her hospital bed."

"I know that. But maybe her coach did it," George said.

"Joe Vesella?" Bess exclaimed. "That nice man?"

"He seemed awfully calm about the whole poisoning thing," George said.

"That's because he doesn't have anything to worry about," Bess replied. She turned to Nancy. "I've learned a lot about the rules from talking to the skaters. If Kerri doesn't skate in this competition, she'll probably get a bye to the nationals."

"A bye?" Nancy asked.

"That means the judges will vote to let her advance to the next level of competition because she's a previous national champion," Bess explained. "So it's probably easier for her if she *doesn't* skate. That way she'll get some rest."

"Then maybe the least likely suspect in the world poisoned Kerri—and you," George said.

Bess leaned forward. "Who?"

"Kerri Welch," George replied.

# 8

## Death Drops

"Kerri Welch did *not* poison herself," Bess said. "No way."

George sighed and turned to Nancy. "You think I'm right, don't you, Nan?"

Nancy looked thoughtful. "I think your hunch makes sense," she told George. "But there's one problem. Kerri almost died."

"Maybe she miscalculated the dose," George suggested.

Nancy shook her head. "If she wanted to avoid competing, there are a million easier ways to do it. She could fake a leg injury, the flu, anything."

"That's true," George admitted. "I guess it wouldn't make sense for her to poison herself."

"It was a good idea, though." Nancy moved

78

toward the bathroom. "Okay. I have *got* to take a shower. See you in the morning."

"You tossed and turned all night," George told Nancy when she woke up the next morning.

Nancy yawned. "I know. I was having nightmares about this case. What time is it?"

"Almost nine," George replied. "I bought some bagels when I went out to run."

Nancy groaned and got out of bed. "I can't believe I overslept."

"The competition starts this morning," Bess said as she munched on a bagel with cream cheese. "Ice dancing is first."

"I'd like to see Scott and Amanda skate their short program this afternoon, but I think I'll skip the ice dancing," Nancy said. "I want to visit Kerri during morning visiting hours."

"I'll go to the hospital with you," Bess said. "I want to say hi to Kerri, too. I hope she's awake."

Taking a cinnamon bagel from the plate, Nancy agreed with her friend. She had plenty of questions to ask Kerri.

"I wonder if Kerri knows she was poisoned?" Bess said an hour later as she and George followed Nancy down the hospital corridor, which smelled of maple syrup, orange juice, and disinfectant.

Nancy was busy looking at room numbers. "Kerri's in four fifty-one, and it just skipped from

79

four twenty-nine to four seventy-five." She stopped a passing nurse. "Excuse me, could you tell us where to find room four fifty-one?"

The nurse smiled. "So you're here to visit the famous skater. She's very popular this morning." He pointed around the corner and down the hall. "It's the room with the police guard at the door."

Nancy exchanged a look with Bess and George. The police must have thought Kerri was in danger.

"May I see a photo ID?" a solemn-looking police officer asked Nancy when she told him she was there to visit Kerri.

"Sure." Nancy flipped open her wallet to show him her driver's license, and he wrote her name on a clipboard. As he added Bess's and George's names, Nancy stole a brief, upside-down glance at the list of people who had already visited Kerri this morning. One entry on the long roster jumped out at her—Meg Abbott.

Nancy walked into the room ahead of Bess and George. Kerri was sleeping. Bess tiptoed around the dresser and inspected the flower arrangements Kerri had received. She pointed to one especially beautiful crystal vase of long-stemmed pink roses. "These are from Meg," she whispered.

Nancy raised her eyebrows. Kerri said she and Meg didn't get along. So why would Meg visit her and send her expensive flowers?

Nancy glanced toward Kerri's medical chart. She knew the information it contained was supposed to be confidential. But what the doctors had written might hold important clues about the case.

"Go for it, Nan," George whispered, reading Nancy's mind.

"Maybe I will sneak a peek," Nancy said. She quietly lifted the chart holder. Bess and George peered over her shoulder, trying to make out the handwriting.

"I can't even read her name, let alone what's wrong with her," Bess said. "And look at all these abbreviations. I give up."

"Wait!" George exclaimed in a whisper. She pointed at a word on the page. "Does that say 'atropine'?"

Nancy nodded. "Great catch, George."

"Is atropine a poison?" Bess asked.

"Yes, a deadly one," Nancy said, furrowing her brow.

Bess shivered. "So Kerri—and I—were poisoned with atropine."

Nancy shook her head, squinting at the chart. "No. I'm pretty sure it says here that the *doctor* is giving Kerri atropine."

Bess looked bewildered. "Why?"

Nancy hung the chart back on the foot of Kerri's bed. "I don't know, but I certainly plan to find out."

Smiling at the police officer and a man in a navy blue blazer, who had just arrived to visit Kerri, she left the room with Bess and George.

"I also want to find out why Meg visited Kerri if they had such a big falling out," Nancy said as they waited for the elevator.

"How are you going to do that?" George asked.

"I think the library would be a good place to start," Nancy said.

Twenty minutes later they took seats in the periodicals section of the library's downtown branch. Nancy flipped through a current *Reader's Guide to Periodical Literature,* looking for listings of articles about Meg or Kerri. Bess and George skimmed through a stack of sports magazines.

"I found something, Nan," George whispered. She held up a photo of a younger Meg, standing on a podium and smiling as a medal was placed around her neck. The headline read: "Silver Lining for Skating's Golden Girl."

Bess listened as Nancy quietly read aloud from the sports magazine. " 'A three-time national champion, Meg Abbott was heavily favored to win the Olympic gold in Calgary. But a disappointing performance resulted in the silver medal. Abbott was then forced into early retirement following the diagnosis of glaucoma, a chronic eye condition that could eventually cause blindness.' "

"I didn't know that," Bess murmured. "Poor Meg."

" 'Abbott turned to coaching and was once again a gold medal favorite, this time as coach to promising skating newcomer Kerri Welch,' " Nancy continued. " 'But after a bitter split, Welch began training with rival coach Joe Vesella and later that year won the national championship.' "

Bess sighed. "That's so sad. Meg put all that work into training Kerri, and then she didn't get any of the credit when Kerri won."

George nodded. "But the rest of the article is positive. It talks about Sarah and how Meg thinks *she* might be the next national champion."

"I bet Meg will be crushed if Sarah doesn't win," Bess said.

"I bet you're right," Nancy agreed.

"Wait till you see this." George reached over Nancy's shoulder and flipped to the last page of the article, which was continued at the back of the magazine. She pointed to a small black-and-white picture.

Nancy looked at a photo of Meg with a handsome, middle-aged gentleman. "That's the man in the blazer who visited Kerri at the hospital this morning."

"Barry Russo," George said. "Meg's agent. He represents a lot of hotshot athletes, and he got Meg the job as the Dynosour Juice spokesperson."

"Russo?" Nancy repeated. "As in Mr. Russo?"

George snapped her fingers. "The guy in the hotel room next to ours. Meg is one of his clients. She *has* to be the person who broke into our room, Nan. She had the means and the opportunity."

83

"And the lipstick," Bess chimed in.

"Okay, okay," Nancy said. "I agree with you. But I'm still a little iffy about her motive."

"Money," Bess said simply. "She doesn't have much, and she wants to get her hands on Uncle Henry's—wherever it is."

Nancy glanced down at the photo. "You know, I would bet Barry Russo is Kerri's agent, too."

"He is," George said. "It says so right here in the article."

Nancy looked thoughtful. "I wonder if Meg knows that Kerri's the new Dynosour Juice spokesperson? And if Mr. Russo got Kerri Meg's old job, where does that leave Meg?"

George shrugged. "Out of luck, I guess."

Nancy nodded. "And maybe with a big reason to want Kerri Welch out of her way. The two women have had similar careers, but Kerri seems to be rising to the top."

"Wow," said George. "You're absolutely right."

Nancy looked at her watch. "We're cutting it pretty close if we want to see all the pairs skate. I just want to check one more thing before we leave, okay?"

Nancy hurried to the reference section. She found the shelf containing medical texts and pulled down the *Physicians' Desk Reference.* "This has everything on prescription drugs," she said. George held the heavy book open as Nancy looked up atropine in the index, then turned to the right page.

"It says here it's a lethal poison," Nancy said, scanning the page. "But in small quantities it can be used as an *antidote* to other toxins. That must be why the doctors were giving it to Kerri." Nancy jotted down the short list of poisons atropine could be used to counteract.

She flipped to the *P* section to look up the first of these, pilocarpine. Nancy's eyes widened as she read the entry aloud: " 'When ingested orally, pilocarpine causes symptoms similar to food poisoning. Harmless when used topically. Found in eye drops typically prescribed for certain types of glaucoma.' "

# 9

## Spiraling Out of Control

George closed the book with a thump. "Meg has glaucoma, and we saw Ted at the drugstore getting a new prescription filled for her. No wonder she needed a refill, if she used her eyedrops to poison Kerri's drink."

"And no wonder Meg went to the hospital to visit Kerri," Bess added. "Meg almost killed her. She must feel guilty." Bess paused. "On the other hand, maybe Meg doesn't feel guilty at all. Maybe she was trying to finish off Kerri so she could get back her old job as the Dynosour Juice spokesperson. And make sure Sarah wins the competition."

"Whoa," Nancy said. "I agree Meg looks pretty suspicious, but we don't know anything for sure." She looked at George. "Scott's mother is a pharmacist, remember? So I'm sure it would have been easy for him to learn about the effects of pilocarpine. And as Meg's student, I bet Scott had easy access to her eyedrops, and lipstick, for that matter. So did Sarah. Either one of them could be guilty."

"But I still think Meg's the one," George said. "Kerri told us Meg would do anything to win. And according to the article I read, the one thing she wants more than anything is for Sarah to win."

"Meg, Scott, and Sarah *all* want Sarah to win," Nancy pointed out.

"Which would be easier with Kerri out of the way." Bess shaded her eyes as they stepped out into the glaring midday sunshine.

Nancy tapped her watch. "Come on, guys. We're late."

Bess sighed and began to drag her feet. "Have a little sympathy. Some of us are still recovering from being poisoned, you know."

"We know. You'll have plenty of time to rest when we get to the arena," George said, giving her cousin a friendly pat on the back.

"You're all heart, George," Bess grumbled.

As the announcer welcomed the crowd to the Crystal Palace, Nancy held up the rope to the reserved section of the bleachers and ducked under it behind Bess and George. Alison was busy supervising the competition, but she had reserved seats for them in the third row.

"See, George?" Bess said. "We're not late at all."

"Excuse me," George murmured as she crossed in front of Scott's family.

Nancy thanked Mrs. Ogden for her advice about Bess's medicine.

"Did the medication help?" Mrs. Ogden asked Bess.

"Oh, yes," Bess said politely. "I feel great. At least, I will once I take a seat." She slid down the bleachers several feet and sat with a contented sigh.

Sarah and Meg slipped into the row in front of them. Sarah was holding a box of food from the snack bar. She handed Meg a hot dog and a bottle of water, then greeted Nancy, Bess, and George.

"Are you ready for your short program tomorrow?" Nancy asked.

Sarah drew in a deep breath. "I hope so. I'm not too nervous about the short. It's the long on Sunday that scares me to death. Four minutes on the ice and five triple jumps." Sarah shivered slightly. "Yikes." Meg gave her a reassuring pat on the shoulder.

"Do you know yet whether Kerri will be competing?" George asked.

Sarah shook her head as she squeezed mustard on her hot dog. "But I hope she does. I want to win this title fair and square. She's my main competition, and I always work harder when she's there."

"We visited Kerri in the hospital this morning," Nancy said casually. "She's doing much better."

Meg shifted uncomfortably on the wooden seat, looking away from Nancy. "Is she? That's great."

So Meg wasn't going to volunteer that she had visited Kerri today, Nancy thought. She *was* trying to hide something.

Over the P.A. system came the announcement that the skaters' five-minute warm-up period would begin.

Bess leaned forward on her elbows as the first group of competitors took the ice. "Amanda's costume is gorgeous!" she cried.

Nancy nodded in agreement, admiring the stunning royal blue design, which was spangled with a smattering of sequins. A filmy skirt secured at the waist with a jeweled button highlighted the high-fashion effect. Scott wore a crisp tuxedo with a blue bow tie and cummerbund.

The pair began to do their practice jumps. Meg drew in a deep breath. Amanda had stumbled coming out of her double axel.

"If she does that in the competition, I'll kill her," Sarah said fiercely.

George raised her eyebrows at Nancy. "I hope that was just a figure of speech," she murmured.

The crowd grew quiet with anticipation as the warm-up period ended and the skaters left the ice in a single line. A minute later the announcer's voice boomed over the P.A. system: "Our first pair, from Minneapolis, Minnesota, and skating out of our very own Crystal Palace—Amanda

Choi and Scott Ogden!" The crowd applauded wildly.

Heads down, Amanda and Scott stroked to the center of the ice. They stood facing each other, Amanda's arms wrapped around Scott's waist. Though they smiled broadly, Nancy could see they were nervous.

A violin sounded the dramatic first note of the skaters' music. "This is it," Bess whispered.

Nancy saw Meg cross her fingers as seconds later Scott and Amanda launched into their side-by-side double axels.

The crowd clapped and cheered as both skaters landed flawlessly. "Yes!" Meg shouted, pumping her fists.

"This is the best I've ever seen them skate," George whispered to Nancy as Scott and Amanda glided effortlessly from one element of their program to another. In one breathtaking move Scott lifted Amanda a few feet off the ice and threw her entire weight away from him, sending her spinning through three revolutions in the air to a perfect landing on one foot. Amanda grinned in relief, floating out of the jump with her arms extended gracefully behind her.

Bess watched intently as Scott grasped Amanda's wrists and propelled her in a circle around him, her body parallel to the ice.

"That's called a death spiral," George said.

"Nice name," Bess said.

The music quickened dramatically, and Scott heaved Amanda into an upright position. The crowd gasped, and a horrified expression crossed Amanda's face. She dropped her hands to her waist, but it was too late. Amanda's skirt lay in a heap around her feet, ready to trip her.

# 10

## Skirting the Issue

Amanda jumped over her skirt as if it were on fire. A few quick steps, and she and Scott managed to get back in time to the music. They executed a tricky footwork sequence that led them to the other side of the rink.

The program built to a dramatic conclusion as Amanda slid across the ice on her knees, coming to rest in front of Scott. As the music ended, she gazed lovingly into his eyes.

The audience leaped to its feet and burst into wild applause. Some people threw flowers and stuffed animals onto the ice. Amanda skated to the edge of the rink, waving at the crowd as she bent to retrieve the gifts.

Nancy noticed that Sarah did not join in the standing ovation. Instead, as Scott and Amanda skated off the ice holding hands, she stalked out of the arena.

"I thought Sarah wanted them to do well," Bess said.

"Well, she doesn't look too happy about it now," George said.

Meg joined Amanda and Scott in the designated area by the barrier as they waited for their scores to be posted. Nancy, Bess, and George had a good view of the skaters and their coach and could hear them discuss the performance.

"Beautiful throw triple salchow," Meg told them. She squeezed Amanda's hand. "That was a great recovery out there."

The crowd booed as the announcer read Scott and Amanda's scores for technical merit, but Meg didn't look displeased by the mediocre marks. She smiled as the artistic marks were posted. "That's more like it," she said. "See? You're still in the running. Skate a clean long program on Saturday, and I guarantee you'll finish in the top three."

Amanda threw her arms around Scott. "I knew we could do it!"

Scott's dark eyes flitted back and forth as he scanned the crowd. "Where's Sarah?" he asked Meg, pulling out of Amanda's embrace.

Meg rubbed her eyes wearily. "I don't know. She walked out a minute ago."

As the next pair skated to the center of the rink, Pete came up to Amanda with the skirt and button from her costume. Amanda thanked him. She examined the fabric and Nancy saw her discreetly touch the waist of her leotard. Did Amanda think her costume had been sabotaged? Nancy wondered. Why else would her skirt fall off in the middle of a competition?

After two more pairs had skated, Scott left his seat to look for Sarah. They returned together about half an hour later, holding hands. Nancy saw the hurt look in Amanda's eyes when she turned to see Scott and Sarah sitting several rows behind her.

By the time the last pair had completed its short program, Choi and Ogden stood in a respectable fourth place.

"The long program on Saturday counts more than the short program toward the total score," George said, "so if they skate well, I'm sure they'll move up in the standings."

After the scores were announced, Amanda stood up and hurried off toward the women's locker room. Nancy got up and motioned for Bess and George to follow her. She wanted to get a good look at Amanda's costume.

In the locker room Nancy congratulated several of the young women, most of whom had already changed out of their skating costumes. Many were talking and laughing as if they were old friends.

Bess finally found Amanda unbraiding her thick, dark hair in front of a mirror. She had changed into an oversize sweatshirt and leggings.

"I'm so glad you're here," Amanda said when she spotted Nancy. She strode over to her locker and twirled the combination lock. "There's no way this was an accident. Sarah sews all the time. You have to figure out what she did to make my costume fall apart." Amanda removed her costume from the locker, and Nancy took it from her shaking hands.

"I knew something didn't feel right when I put my costume on. I thought I was imagining things," Amanda said. "The skirt seemed too tight. But it was fine at my last fitting. And no, I did not gain weight."

Bess fingered the loose threads that had held the button in place. Next to them she spotted two tiny holes. "Somebody moved the button."

"Are you sure?" Nancy asked Bess.

Bess nodded. "Look, it's only a teeny difference, enough to make the skirt fit a little snugly. Except that when Amanda made a sudden movement, the strain was enough to make the button pop off."

"Which is why my skirt fell down." Amanda scowled. "I knew it. I've put up with a lot, but that's it. Sarah's going to pay for this."

"Are you sure Sarah did this?" Nancy asked Amanda gently.

Amanda's brown eyes flashed. "Of course. She wants me to quit so she can have Scott all to herself. Well, she's not going to get her way. I don't care what stunt Sarah pulls next." Amanda gulped back a sob. "I'll show her, and I'll show Meg. I won't let her destroy everything I've worked for."

Bess put a hand on Amanda's shoulder. "I'm glad you're not going to quit. I really admire your determination."

"I'm sure Scott does, too," Nancy added. "He couldn't skate without you."

Amanda looked surprised. "Sure, he could. If I were out of the picture, Sarah would be skating with him again like that." She snapped her fingers.

George frowned. "But I thought Sarah wanted to quit pairs to concentrate on singles."

"She did." Amanda sighed. "But it was mostly Meg's idea. Now that Sarah's seen what it's like to have Scott skate with someone else, she's changed her mind."

"But Meg hasn't," Nancy guessed.

Amanda nodded. "Right. And as long as Sarah does well in singles and Scott has an okay partner, Meg's not going to make any changes."

"You're not just okay," Bess said. "You and Scott were terrific today."

"Thanks." Amanda stretched her ponytail holder nervously between her fingers. "Scott and I can have a great partnership. There's chemistry between us. I'm so much better for him than Sarah is. He's going to figure that out someday."

Amanda stood up and moved back to the mirror as Nancy exchanged a look with Bess and George.

"Congratulations on your skating today, Amanda. We'll let you know as soon as we find out anything," Nancy said, motioning for Bess and George to follow her out of the room.

"Wow," Bess said as soon as the locker room door swung closed behind them. "Amanda really *is* trying to steal Scott away from Sarah."

Nancy sighed. "Just what we need. One more suspect."

George raised her eyebrows. "Amanda?"

Nancy nodded. "Amanda may not like Sarah, but she sure has a good reason for wanting her to win the competition. Amanda said it herself—the better Sarah does in singles, the more likely it is that Amanda can keep skating with Scott."

"And maybe become his new girlfriend," Bess added. "At least, that's what Amanda seems to think."

"We already know Amanda isn't exactly Kerri's biggest fan," George observed. "Amanda didn't like sharing a coach with her, remember? And she could have gotten to Meg's eyedrops just as easily as Scott or Sarah. I see what you're saying, Nan. Maybe *Amanda* poisoned Kerri to increase Sarah's chances of winning the competition—and her own chances of staying with Scott."

Nancy nodded. "There's another thing. If what Amanda says is true—if Sarah wants to start skating with Scott again—that explains something that was bothering me before. I didn't understand why Sarah might try to hurt Amanda with the

Zamboni if it would leave Scott without a pairs partner. But if Sarah's planning to pick up where she left off as Scott's partner, Amanda's Zamboni accident wouldn't harm Scott's skating career at all. And it would put Sarah exactly where she wants to be."

Amanda exited the locker room with her duffel bag. As the door closed behind her, Alison approached from the opposite direction.

"I was just looking for you," Alison said to Amanda. "I was really impressed by your program. But what happened with the skirt?"

"I am positive that Sarah ruined my costume on purpose," Amanda said firmly.

Alison looked skeptical. "How could she have done that? I'm sure Sarah doesn't have your locker combination."

"You keep a master sheet with all the combinations in your office, right?" Amanda asked Alison, who nodded. "Sarah was in there the other day, supposedly watching her skating tape," Amanda continued. "She could've looked at your list then."

Alison turned pale. "I guess you might be right. Oh, Amanda, if that's true, I'm very sorry. I'll have all the combinations changed right away."

"Thanks." The arena lights dimmed. "I'd better find Meg before the arena closes," Amanda said, waving as she moved off toward the lobby.

"This is getting worse and worse." Alison's voice trembled as she looked after Amanda. "It took Uncle Henry years to establish the Crystal Palace's reputation, and now everything is falling apart in no time."

"Alison, I know your uncle would be very proud of you," Nancy said. "I heard lots of positive comments about the competition today."

George and Bess nodded. "The Crystal Palace is the nicest arena I've ever seen," George said. "I've been dying to get out on that ice since the minute we got here."

"Really?" Alison managed a small smile as she glanced at her watch. "You know, the arena is closed now so the ice can be resurfaced before the senior women's practice tonight. And since there are two rinks and only one Zamboni . . ."

George grinned. "Are you saying we can skate?"

"If you don't mind a few rough patches, why not? I'll even throw in free skate rentals out of the kindness of my heart."

Nancy, Bess, and George followed Alison to the skate rental desk at the front of the arena. Alison unlocked the door and located suitable skate boots, half a size smaller than the teens' normal shoe sizes.

Nancy laced up her boots first, double tying the long laces at the top. She wobbled over to the hockey rink in her skates and tentatively stepped onto the ice, skidding a little as she let go of the barrier. After half a lap she was skating confidently. She cut over toward the middle of the rink.

Almost as if she were skating on pebbles, Nancy felt the ice become rough under her feet. She put out her arms to steady herself, but it was too late. Nancy's right skate hit something hard, and she went flying through the air.

# 11

## *Shattered*

Facedown on the ice, Nancy struggled to push herself upright. "Ow!" she cried as she felt something sharp sting her palms.

"Don't move, Nan!" George shouted, and skated rapidly toward the middle of the rink.

"I'm going to get Alison," Bess called. She tugged off her skates and hurried through the lobby.

"Careful," Nancy told George. "There are tiny pieces of glass all over the ice."

George helped Nancy to her feet and led her toward Alison's nearby office to clean her bleeding palms.

"You're lucky you didn't hurt yourself badly," George said.

"I was skating pretty slowly. But if one of the

competitors had hit that broken glass during a jump or spin, she would have taken a terrible fall."

George opened the door to Alison's office. "Just what this competition needs. Another so-called accident. Where did that glass come—"

George stopped in midsentence as she and Nancy glimpsed the luminous Monet print near Alison's window. The picture was slashed into tatters, the wooden frame destroyed.

George cleared her throat. "I guess that answers my question."

Nancy shook her head in disgust. She made her way into Alison's bathroom, rinsed out her cuts, and checked them for small fragments of glass.

As Nancy threw away her paper towel, she spotted a bandage wrapper in the trash can. "I don't think I'm the only person who cut herself on broken glass from this painting," she told George. "I bet we find our suspect wearing a bandage."

Alison hurried into her office, followed by Bess. She gasped when she saw the ruined print.

"It wasn't a valuable piece of artwork, was it?" Nancy asked Alison gently.

Alison shook her head. "No, just an inexpensive reproduction. But it was one of my favorites— *Floating Ice*. I was looking at it today . . . thinking how calm and peaceful it made me feel."

"When was that?" Nancy asked.

"Late this morning. I haven't been in my office since." Alison's voice became angry. "If I thought it did any good, I certainly would have made sure to keep the door locked."

Ted poked his head into the room. He carried a broom and dustpan, and heavy gloves protected his hands from the shards of glass he had been removing from the ice. His mouth fell open when he saw the painting. "Is this where the broken glass came from?"

"It would seem so," Alison said with a sigh. "How's the cleanup coming?"

"Pete and I have everything under control."

Alison smiled. "Thanks, Ted. I knew I could count on you."

Ted looked to Nancy. "Any idea who's behind this latest incident?"

Nancy shook her head. "Not yet."

"I think I have an idea. You said the skaters are supposed to practice tonight, right?" George asked Alison.

Alison nodded.

Bess handed Nancy two bandages from her bulging purse and said, "There are several skaters who could still beat Sarah—like Dominique Morrow. She's skating really well."

George nodded. "Sarah—or Amanda, or Meg, or Scott—could have put the glass on the ice to get rid of Sarah's competition."

Nancy tore open a bandage wrapper. "Wait a minute. You said the Zamboni was going to resurface the ice before the practices tonight."

Alison nodded slowly. "That's true."

"Then this whole line of reasoning doesn't make sense. I'm sure Sarah and the other skaters knew that's why the arena was closed," Nancy continued. "And they must have realized the Zamboni would sweep the glass away before anyone skated on it."

"You're right, Nan," Alison said. "If the Zamboni didn't get a flat tire first from running over the glass. Yikes." She shuddered. "I would have been in a terrible situation if that happened. Getting Zamboni parts is a nightmare. When nonessential parts go bad, we don't even bother to try to replace them."

"I guess it's a good thing I discovered the glass, then," Nancy said, smoothing the second bandage across her palm.

"Not to make light of your accident, Nan," Alison said, "but you saved me from major misfortune."

"Glad I could be of service," Nancy commented wryly.

As they returned to the lobby, Nancy saw that Pete and a few other workers had almost finished cleaning the glass from the ice. Pete was left-handed, Nancy noted as she watched him work.

The rink reopened just before the competitors returned for their evening practice.

"It's only eight o'clock, and I'm exhausted," Bess said a short while later as they entered their hotel room. She collapsed on the foot of her bed.

George sat on the other end of the bed and pulled open the nightstand drawer. "Where did the room-service menu go?"

Bess limply raised her hand and pointed toward the dresser. "Over there."

As Nancy moved aside a stack of files to uncover the menu, a piece of paper fluttered to the ground. "What's this?" she asked, bending to pick it up. Meg's name was scrawled across the back of a snack bar receipt.

Bess opened one eye. "Meg's autograph," she explained. "I got it yesterday when she was in a good mood."

Nancy studied Meg's neat, up-and-down handwriting. It looked nothing like the slanted letters of the threatening lipstick message on the mirror. Of course, Meg could have been trying to disguise her writing, Nancy reasoned.

She opened the menu and said, "What's for dinner?"

Half an hour later Nancy dipped a mozzarella stick in tomato sauce as she used her other hand to flip a page of Henry MacDonald's endless files.

Bess peeled a crisp piece of pepperoni from her pizza slice and popped it in her mouth. "Any luck with the files?"

Nancy sighed. "Nope. How about you, George?"

"Earth to George!" Bess waved a hand in front of George's face. Her cousin stared intently at the basketball game on the television set.

"Hey." George brushed away Bess's arm. "It's the fourth quarter."

"It's a commercial," Bess said as the score flashed across the screen and loud music blared from the television set.

"Next, a Channel Eleven News exclusive," said a newscaster in a dramatic voice. "An interview with figure skater Kerri Welch. She'll tell us all about the disaster at the Crystal Palace."

Nancy, Bess, and George all froze in place, speechless for a moment.

Then Nancy said, "Kerri must have talked to the press about the poisoning. That must be the 'disaster' at the arena."

"Oh, no," George said.

"Poor Alison," Bess added.

Nancy stared grimly at the TV. The case had just taken a turn for the worse. And she desperately wanted to help her friend, before the Crystal Palace and all it meant to Alison shattered into countless pieces.

# 12

## One Mystery Solved

Nancy was reading the sports section of the news-paper and Bess was in the shower when the phone rang early the next morning. Nancy snatched up the receiver. "Hello?"

"Hi, Nan. It's Alison. Did I wake you?"

"No. I was just reading Kerri's interview in the paper."

Nancy heard Alison sigh. "Thanks to Kerri, the whole world knows about the problems at the Crystal Palace. Did you see the Channel Eleven News last night?"

"I'm afraid so," Nancy said.

"Well," Alison said lightly, "Kerri sure knows how to make the most of being poisoned. All this publicity will do wonders for her career."

"Too bad it has to be at your expense." Nancy kept her voice level, but she couldn't hide the anger she felt toward Kerri. In her news interviews the skater had exaggerated the incidents at the Crystal Palace and made Alison seem incompetent. Kerri was probably acting on the advice of her agent, Nancy thought. She reminded herself that she needed to have a talk with Mr. Russo.

"Whatever I think of Kerri, I truly *am* glad she's recovered enough to compete today," Alison said.

"Me, too." Nancy glanced down at the newspaper article she was holding. "It's amazing, considering that she was poisoned not just once, but twice." The article told how Kerri had ingested two different poisons. "I guess Kerri is lucky to come out of this as well as she did," Nancy added.

"I know," Alison said. "I can't believe she was poisoned at the Crystal Palace, and then in her hospital room! The poor girl . . . I wonder how it happened. Didn't you say there was a police officer guarding Kerri's door?"

"Yes, but he didn't exactly watch our every move when we were visiting," Nancy said.

Alison laughed. "I'm sure. Otherwise you never would have taken a peek at Kerri's medical files and figured out that she was poisoned by Meg's eyedrops."

"Meg visited Kerri in the hospital, too," Nancy pointed out.

"So Meg had the chance to poison Kerri both times—at the rink and in her hospital room," Alison said.

Nancy shifted the phone to her other ear. "But if Meg's the poisoner, she must be pretty daring, or else unbelievably stupid. I mean, the police know she visited Kerri. She had to sign in before seeing Kerri. They know Kerri was poisoned with pilocarpine. They probably also know Meg has glaucoma, and that pilocarpine is a common remedy for it. Meg has to realize she's the number-one suspect."

Alison was silent for a moment. "I agree with you that Meg's too smart to set herself up as the obvious suspect. But who else had the opportunity to poison Kerri twice?"

Nancy ran through the suspects in her mind and finally said, "I don't know. I need to think about it."

"I almost forgot," Alison said. "I have some good news. Ted solved the melting ice problem."

"Great," Nancy said. "What happened?"

"Pete accidentally turned off the compressors. Ted confronted him this morning, and he admitted it was his fault."

"Accidentally? How'd he do that?"

"I'm not sure. But Pete's made a ton of mistakes since he was hired." Alison sighed. "I feel terrible. Pete's such a nice guy, but Ted is going to have to fire him."

"Who hired Pete in the first place?" Nancy asked.

"I did," Alison admitted sheepishly. "Pete had

a wonderful résumé. He was assistant manager for ten years at the Ice Chateau in Northfield. He left only a couple of months ago."

They chatted a few minutes longer, then hung up.

Something was fishy, Nancy thought. If Pete had so much managerial experience at another ice rink, why had he made those mistakes? She vowed to do some checking into his background.

George breezed in from her morning run, her dark curls tousled by the wind. "Guess who I saw in the lobby?"

"Mr. Russo?" Nancy asked hopefully.

George shook her head. "Pete Bradley. I said hi to him, but I don't think he heard me."

Nancy tapped her pencil against the desk. "Something weird is going on with Pete."

Nancy found a listing for the Ice Chateau in the phone book, then dialed the number. She asked to speak with the manager.

"I'm the manager. How can I help you?" the man asked gruffly.

"I'm trying to get some information about Pete Bradley," Nancy began.

"Sorry, can't help you." The man abruptly hung up the phone.

Nancy held the phone away from her ear as the dial tone echoed loudly.

"He hung up on you?" George asked.

Nancy nodded. "I think this definitely calls for a visit to the Ice Chateau."

An hour later Bess sopped up the last bit of syrup on her plate with a piece of soggy French toast.

"Glad to see you're feeling better," Nancy said to her. Nancy gathered papers from the night-stand and asked her friends, "Do you mind if we drop these files off at the Crystal Palace before we head over to the Ice Chateau? Alison said she needed to look at them this morning."

"No problem." George hastily ran a comb through her hair, which was still damp from the shower. "I certainly don't have to be anywhere."

Bess nodded. "Just as long as we're back at the Crystal Palace in time for the women's programs this afternoon. I've been waiting all week to see them skate."

"Women's singles is the most popular event of the whole competition." Nancy crossed her fingers. "Let's hope nothing goes wrong at the Crystal Palace today."

On their way down the hall Nancy knocked on Mr. Russo's door, but there was no answer.

"Maybe he's at the Crystal Palace," George said.

"I hope so," Nancy said. "I can't wait to ask him a few questions about his clients."

But there was no sign of Mr. Russo in the busy

lobby of the Crystal Palace. Scanning the area, Nancy saw Amanda coming out of the pro shop. She was clutching a small paper bag.

"She doesn't look happy," Bess murmured as Amanda approached them.

"Hi. Why aren't you out there on the ice?" Nancy asked Amanda.

"I had to buy another screwdriver at the pro shop. Scott took mine for the third time." Amanda sighed in annoyance. "Well, he swears he didn't this time, but I'm sure it was him, because it disappeared during practice."

Nancy registered this information. So Amanda's screwdriver *was* missing. If the screwdriver really had been stolen, Amanda wasn't the one who dropped it outside Alison's office. But was Amanda telling the truth?

"Anyhow," Amanda continued, "the other reason I'm not practicing is that Scott called me this morning and said he'd be an hour late—again." She scowled. "I don't know what his problem is. I just hope he's able to skate the long program with that gash in his hand."

Nancy exchanged a glance with Bess and George. They were pretty sure the person who smashed Alison's painting had been cut on the broken glass. Was it Scott?

Nancy took a deep breath. "Scott cut his hand? How did that happen?" she asked casually.

Amanda kicked at the barrier with her skate. "Good question. I heard Scott telling Meg he did it practicing lifts with me. But that's not true. And I don't understand why he'd lie."

"Scott *wouldn't* lie unless he had something to hide," Nancy said a few minutes later. She maneuvered the car safely out from between Ted's black convertible and a large van.

"Do you think Scott used Amanda's screwdriver to break into Alison's office and steal Sarah's tape?" George asked.

"Of course not." Bess scoffed. "Why would he steal his girlfriend's video?"

As Nancy guided the car onto the highway, she said, "I have an idea. We've been assuming all along that Scott wants Sarah to win, right?"

"Right," Bess and George replied.

"Well, how do you think Scott would feel if Sarah skated badly? *And* if he and Amanda also skated badly?"

"Pretty depressed," George said.

"Maybe," Nancy agreed. "Or maybe that's exactly what Scott wants. If he could get Sarah and Meg to change their minds about Sarah's quitting pairs—"

"Then Scott and Sarah could skate together again!" Bess exclaimed. "I see what you mean, Nan."

"It would definitely help Scott's skating career," George said. "I mean, he and Amanda are good, but from what I hear, he and Sarah were *great*."

"It would make his personal life a lot less

complicated, too," Bess added. "He wouldn't have to worry about all that tension between Sarah and Amanda."

"So Scott may have tried to hurt his own partner. *And* his girlfriend," George said slowly. "Wow."

"And Kerri," Bess added. "As Nancy said, Scott's mother's a pharmacist. It was probably easy for him to find out about Meg's eyedrops."

"Wait," George said to Bess. "If we think Scott was trying to keep Sarah from doing well in the competition, that part doesn't make sense. Kerri's poisoning could have *helped* Sarah. Sarah could have a better chance at winning if Kerri was out of the way."

Nancy shook her head. "Not necessarily. Bess said that if Kerri couldn't skate because of her poisoning, the judges would probably give her a bye to the nationals. I checked it out, and Bess is right. Kerri would actually have had an advantage over Sarah by advancing without having to compete this week. She'd be totally recovered from the poisoning."

"I'm surprised Kerri decided to skate, then," George remarked.

"I'm not," Bess said as Nancy drove into the tiny parking lot at the Ice Chateau, a redbrick building next to a bowling alley. "If Kerri wins, she'll get even more publicity. And if she loses, she can blame it on the poisoning."

114

Bess led the way to the rink. Following her friend, Nancy blinked at what she saw on the ice.

In the middle of the rink, practicing a difficult lift move together, were Scott and Sarah.

# 13

## A Surprising Admission

When he saw Nancy, George, and Bess, Scott's arms buckled, and he set Sarah down on the ice. Nancy beckoned them over to the barrier.

"Hi," Scott said, exchanging a guilty look with Sarah. "I guess our secret's out."

"I guess so," Nancy agreed. "Are you planning to get back together as a pair?"

Sarah nodded. "We're going to skate an exhibition together at the Winter Carnival next month."

"What about Amanda?" Bess asked.

Scott looked uncomfortable. "Amanda's great, but it's not the same as skating with Sarah. Sarah and I were meant to be together."

Sarah looped her arm through Scott's. "We were so miserable not skating with each other. It seemed like an okay idea at first, but it just wasn't

116

working. And when Meg wouldn't let us go back to being partners, we decided we couldn't listen to what she said. Nobody knows this, but we've been practicing here for months."

"Meg's not going to be too happy if she finds out," George said.

"She *is* going to find out," Scott said. "We're going to tell her as soon as sectionals are over. If she won't let us skate together, then we're going to change coaches. We've decided that's the only thing we can do."

"But we want to wait until the right time to tell Meg. I know she needs money pretty badly. If I win this competition, she won't want to lose me as her student, and I think she'll agree to what I ask. And I really do want to stay with Meg. She's a good coach." Sarah turned to Nancy. "That's why I was so glad when you found my tape. Thanks for returning it."

Nancy tried to absorb this new information. "I don't get it," she said. "What in the world does the video have to do with any of this?"

"I taped over most of it, but one of my practice sessions with Scott was on the end of the video," Sarah explained. "If Meg or Amanda had seen it, it would have been a disaster."

"So *that's* why you were so upset when the tape disappeared," Bess said.

117

Sarah nodded. "But I couldn't explain without giving away our secret. I guess you didn't watch the end of the tape, Nancy."

Nancy shook her head. The tape had gone black at the end of Sarah's practice session, and then Alison had rewound it. They hadn't realized there was more footage at the end. Nancy glanced over at Scott, who was massaging the bandage on his hand. "You hurt your hand practicing with Sarah, didn't you?"

"I was careless on a lift, and her blade nicked my hand." Scott looked embarrassed. "I told Meg I cut myself practicing with Amanda. I hope she doesn't find out from Amanda that I lied."

"We just ran into Amanda at the Crystal Palace," Bess said. "She was pretty worried about your hand. It's not going to hurt your performance, is it?"

"I hope not." Scott sighed. "I feel guilty about putting Amanda through this. I'm always late for practice. She must know something's up."

"That day she was almost hurt by the Zamboni, Scott was practicing with me," Sarah explained. "He felt terrible that he wasn't at the Crystal Palace when he should have been."

"Wait a minute!" George exclaimed, looking closely at Sarah. "I was jogging around Lake Calhoun that morning, and I thought I saw Scott skating with Amanda. But it must have been *you*."

"It was." Sarah frowned. "I can't believe you

got us mixed up. Amanda and I don't look anything alike."

"From a distance you do," Nancy said. "And you should be glad. This gives you an alibi. If you were at Lake Calhoun, you couldn't have been driving the Zamboni that almost hit Amanda."

"You thought I might have been driving the Zamboni?" Sarah turned pale. "I would *never* do something like that. Never! Tell them, Scott."

Scott put a protective arm around Sarah. "Sarah knew I was leaving Amanda to train with her. Why would she try and hurt Amanda?"

Nancy looked Scott in the eye. "Who else might have a motive to harm Amanda and destroy her costume?"

"Okay, okay," Sarah blurted out. "I confess. I'm the one who ruined Amanda's costume."

Nancy was startled by Sarah's sudden admission. "You did?"

Sarah looked down at the ice, her cheeks pink. "I'm sorry, Scott," she said softly.

He reached out and took her hands. "Sarah . . . what were you thinking?"

"I wanted you to do well in the competition. Really, I did." Sarah wiped away a tear as it slid down her cheek. "But I saw how well you and Amanda have been skating, and I thought . . . I thought you might change your mind about splitting up with her. She wants a romantic relationship with you, Scott. And if you decided you wanted to be with her instead of me, I don't know what I'd do."

"Sarah, I love *you*." Scott looked deep into her eyes. "You have to believe me. No matter what Amanda does, I'll always love you."

Sarah threw her arms around Scott, choking back sobs. Feeling like an intruder, Nancy turned away. She looked up and was surprised to see tears glistening in Bess's eyes.

Scott and Sarah suddenly remembered they weren't alone. Sarah gratefully took the wad of tissues Bess handed her.

"Nancy, you have to believe that Sarah wasn't the Zamboni driver," Scott said earnestly. "I was with her that morning, I swear. We weren't anywhere near the Crystal Palace."

"All right. But who else might have a motive to harm Amanda?" Nancy asked them.

"I know one person," Sarah said quietly. She hesitated and then said, "Meg."

"Meg?" Bess repeated. "Why would Meg want to hurt her own student?"

"Because she's afraid Amanda could hurt her first," Scott replied evenly. He glanced at Sarah. "Sarah and I have talked about this, and it bothers us a lot. Meg's the only person we can think of who might have a reason to threaten Amanda."

"And what would that reason be?" Nancy asked him.

Scott sighed. "It's no accident that Amanda and I skate so well together," he explained reluctantly.

"Meg saw us perform in an exhibition a few years ago, and she knew we would click. So she went to *a lot* of trouble to talk Amanda into leaving her old coach."

"Oh." George nodded. "I see."

"That's considered a serious ethical violation by the professional figure skaters' association," Sarah explained to Nancy and Bess. "If Amanda tells anyone Meg recruited her away from her old coach, Meg could lose her professional rating. That would damage Meg's career."

"But Amanda wouldn't do that," Bess said. "Would she?"

Sarah rolled her eyes. "You don't know Amanda very well. She hates training with Meg. She only puts up with it because of Scott. But Amanda's threatened to report Meg to the association lots of times."

"Meg deserves to be reported if she's capable of pulling stunts like the one with the Zamboni," George declared.

"I know." Scott frowned. "To tell you the truth, I still have a hard time believing she could have done that. I know Meg would never really hurt anyone. Maybe she just wanted to scare Amanda a little."

"Unfortunately, Amanda doesn't get the hint too easily." Sarah tossed her long hair and caught it at the nape of her neck with her gold barrette.

Nancy elbowed Bess, glancing at the distinctive barrette. Sarah might have an alibi, but that still didn't explain why Nancy had found a barrette matching hers near the runaway Zamboni.

"What a beautiful barrette!" Bess exclaimed on cue. "Where in the world did you get it?"

Sarah shrugged. "It's not mine."

"Really? Whose is it? I've never seen anything like it. I'd love to buy one."

Sarah snapped the barrette closed over her thick ponytail. "It's Meg's."

# 14

## The Truth, At Last

Nancy hid her reaction to the news. Until now, she'd thought Scott and Sarah's theory that Meg was threatening Amanda seemed far-fetched. But now there was evidence to back it up. Nancy herself had found the matching barrette near the Zamboni.

Nancy remembered the look of fear in Amanda's eyes that morning, and her reluctance to tell Nancy who might be trying to hurt her. And she had seen the barrette that Nancy found next to the Zamboni. Surely she had recognized it as Meg's.

Nancy also remembered what Amanda had said in the locker room after discovering that someone had tampered with her skirt. She had promised she would "show Meg and Sarah." At the time Nancy thought Amanda just meant she was determined to keep skating well, but maybe it was some kind of hidden threat—the kind of threat Sarah and Scott said she'd been making against Meg for months. Maybe Meg was now taking drastic action to prevent Amanda from carrying it out.

"Meg has great taste," Nancy commented, pretending to admire the barrette in Sarah's hair.

"I guess." Sarah clasped her hand around it. "This was a birthday gift, though."

"And she gave it to you?" Bess said. "That's awfully nice."

Sarah laughed. "Not really. She was just irritated because my hair was always falling in my face at practice. Anyhow, she has another barrette just like this one. They were a pair."

So there *was* another barrette, Nancy thought. And it had been in Meg's possession until somebody dropped it on the ice at the Crystal Palace and Nancy picked it up. But did Meg drop it? Or was somebody trying to set her up?

Sarah looked at her watch. "Scott, we've got to get to the Crystal Palace." She sat on a bench and began to unlace her skates.

"Can you guys do us a favor and keep our secret for a few more days?" Scott asked, his eyes pleading. "We promise we'll tell Meg and Amanda we're skating together as soon as the competition's over."

"All right," Nancy agreed, "in exchange for a small piece of information. Do you know Pete Bradley from the Crystal Palace?"

Scott and Sarah nodded.

"You said you've been working out here at the Ice Chateau for a few months. Was Pete the manager here recently?" Nancy asked them.

"No way," Scott said firmly. "We know everybody who works here."

Sarah nodded and said, "Why do you ask?"

Nancy shrugged. "Just a small misunderstanding."

"Not a misunderstanding," George said after Scott and Sarah left. "Pete must have lied on his job application."

Nancy nodded. "I can't wait to get back to the Crystal Palace to look through the personnel files."

"Personnel files?" Alison looked slightly dazed as she hurried through the lobby with an armload of forms and a cup of coffee.

"You look a little swamped," Nancy said.

"I'm a lot swamped," Alison replied. "The police have been grilling me all morning about Kerri's poisoning, because it happened at the Crystal Palace. Ted called in sick, Pete's been fired, and I'm about to have that nervous breakdown." She studied Nancy's face. "You look cheery. A new lead?"

"We'll see," Nancy said. "I'll fill you in later. But is it okay if I use your office for a few minutes?"

"Oh, right. The personnel files. Go ahead."

Alison gulped down her coffee. "There's one of the judges. Excuse me . . ." And she rushed off.

"Poor Alison," Bess said. "I bet she'll be glad when this competition's over."

"As long as nothing else goes wrong," George added.

Bess and George set out to look for Meg, and Nancy headed down the hallway toward Alison's office. She was startled to find herself face-to-face with Barry Russo.

"Mr. Russo," she called as he tried to sidestep her. "Mr. Russo!" Nancy strode after him, finally catching up to him just before he reached the lobby. "My name is Nancy Drew. I'm staying in the hotel room next to yours at the Excelsior. I've been trying to talk to you for two days."

Mr. Russo sighed. "Yes, Ms. Drew. I know. I did receive your messages—all five of them."

"Well, I wasn't sure, since you didn't return any of my calls," Nancy said.

"If you'll excuse me, I'm very busy."

"Busy making up stories for Kerri Welch to tell the news media," Nancy said. She knew she had to be tough with Mr. Russo if she was going to get any information from him at all.

"Everything Kerri Welch said in those interviews is one hundred percent true," Mr. Russo stated firmly.

"Of course," Nancy answered. "Are you ready to tell me which of your clients broke into my hotel room? Or maybe it was you."

126

Mr. Russo drew in a deep breath. "Keep this up, Ms. Drew, and I'll sue you for slander."

"You wouldn't have a case," Nancy replied. "Just hear me out, Mr. Russo," she went on. "I'm trying to help your clients by getting to the bottom of this situation before anything else goes wrong. But to do that, I need some help from you."

Mr. Russo's hostile attitude disappeared in an instant. "All right, Ms. Drew. I'll tell you what I know, but it isn't much. None of my clients was alone in my hotel room for a moment. I find it impossible to believe that any of them broke into your room." He paused. "What else would you like to know?"

"I need details about Kerri's poisoning when she was in the hospital," Nancy said. "Do the police have any suspects?"

Mr. Russo looked uncomfortable. "I'll tell you this if you promise not to repeat it to anyone else. The poisoning at the hospital was . . . well, it was part of Kerri's treatment. The doctors gave her some type of toxic drug to counteract the effects of the first poison."

The atropine, Nancy realized. The second "poison" was an antidote to the first one, and it was given to make Kerri well—not to harm her. "In other words," Nancy said, "there was no second attempt on Kerri's life. You were just trying to make the story sound more sensational by stretching the truth."

"Yes . . . no," Mr. Russo said, flustered. "If you

look at the press release I prepared, you will see that the information it contains is strictly factual. She did ingest poison twice."

"But one of the poisons couldn't harm her," Nancy finished. She realized that Russo had failed to mention this fact to the press. "Thank you for your help, Mr. Russo," Nancy said curtly.

Mr. Russo hurried away, and Nancy headed back to Alison's office. She grunted as she lifted a stack of personnel folders from Alison's cabinet. Of all the files in Alison's office, these were among the few she hadn't yet examined. Résumés and work evaluations had not seemed likely to have much bearing on the location of Henry MacDonald's missing money. But Nancy felt she had to be thorough on a case as difficult as this one.

Nancy found Pete's folder toward the top of the stack. Inside the file was a page of interview notes in Alison's familiar handwriting. The next page was Pete's résumé. Nancy read a note in the margin from Ted to Alison. It said that the manager at the Ice Chateau had given Pete a glowing recommendation. But that couldn't be true, Nancy thought. Pete had never worked at the Ice Chateau. So either the manager was lying . . . or Ted was.

Ted had been working closely with Pete, Nancy realized. If Ted was such a good assistant manager, why hadn't he noticed Pete's lack of experience? And what if Pete had made more mistakes Alison wasn't even aware of? Nancy wondered. It was definitely possible. What if Pete's incompetence was costing Alison money?

Nancy pulled out all the files relating to the Crystal Palace's budget. Almost immediately she saw a requisition signed by Pete last month for new headlights for the Zamboni. Nancy looked at the order blank closely and saw Ted's initials, verifying that the headlights had been delivered. But hadn't Alison said that nonessential parts for the Zamboni were rarely ordered? A Zamboni could be operated without headlights in a lit arena. But the person who tried to run down Amanda needed them, Nancy thought. Because the driver of the Zamboni had to work under cover of darkness.

Nancy came across the canceled check Alison's uncle had written to Waterworks, Inc., the year before for the mystery repairs at the rink. She gasped in recognition as she noticed the amount on the check. Flipping through another file, she found the large payment Ted had made to Waterworks to have the pipes under the ice repaired. She'd thought that figure looked familiar! The amounts on both checks were exactly the same. They must have been for the same repair work.

Nancy drew in a deep breath. Based on this information, she would bet that Henry MacDonald had had the pipes under the ice fixed only last year. That's what the mystery repairs were. Why did Ted do them all over again?

Nancy wished there were some way she could

contact Mr. Peters from Waterworks. She stared in frustration at the company's business card, with its now useless address and phone number. The owner's name jumped out at her. Mr. Bradley Peters, Sr. . . . Mr. Brad Peters . . . Pete Bradley!

Nancy grew excited. The man who had worked at the Crystal Palace under the name Pete Bradley very possibly wasn't Pete Bradley at all. Nancy was willing to bet that he was actually Bradley Peters, Jr., the son of the owner of Waterworks.

Someone had hired Brad Peters to create chaos at the Crystal Palace—to turn off the compressors, to make scheduling errors, to trip the circuit breaker while someone else drove the Zamboni . . . Now Nancy remembered Alison's saying that Brad Peters, Jr., worked at the Excelsior Hotel. He probably had a master key. He must have been the one who broke into Nancy's room!

Nancy felt a sinking sensation in the pit of her stomach. Only one person could have planned this elaborate scheme. Who had recommended Pete to Alison? Who had suggested that Nancy stay at the Excelsior Hotel? Who had the knowledge and the opportunity to mastermind every act of sabotage that had occurred at the Crystal Palace? Ted Marler. But why?

Nancy's racing thoughts were interrupted by the sound of a rap on the door. It was Bess. She walked into the room along with Meg.

Meg cleared her throat. "Sorry to interrupt you,

Nancy. But Bess said you found something that belongs to me."

Nancy nodded. "Your barrette." She unzipped her handbag and handed the ornate barrette to Meg.

Meg's mouth dropped open. "You found it! I've been looking all over for this. Where was it?"

"On the floor in the arena," Nancy said vaguely.

Meg turned the barrette over and over in her hands. "I can't tell you how happy I am to have this back. It's part of a pair. I lent Sarah the other one."

Nancy smiled. "I take it the barrettes have sentimental value?"

Meg nodded. "They were a birthday gift from Ted. He bought them for me in Spain."

Ted again, Nancy thought.

"I've got to get back to Sarah. Thanks for finding this, Nancy." Meg hurried down the hallway, clutching the barrette in her palm.

"I saved you a seat for the competition, Nan," Bess said over her shoulder. "See you in a half hour, okay?"

Nancy nodded absently and picked up the phone. George had seen Pete in the hotel lobby this morning. That could mean Brad Peters was back at work on his real job at the Excelsior. If she could prove that Pete and Brad were the same person, Nancy decided, she would be certain she was on the right track.

131

Nancy dialed the Excelsior's front desk. "Yes. I'd like to speak with Brad Peters," she said.

"I'm sorry," the clerk replied. "He's at lunch right now. Would you like to leave a message?"

"No, thank you," Nancy said, hanging up the phone. At least she knew Brad Peters was back from his "vacation." But she would have to wait to confirm her suspicions.

Nancy closed her eyes as she reviewed the incidents of the past week. Kerri's poisoning, the attacks on Amanda, the melted ice . . . everything had seemed to revolve around the fierce competition among the skaters. But who had suffered the most as a result of all these mishaps? Alison had, Nancy realized. Alison and the Crystal Palace were hurt each time something happened to the skaters or the arena. Was Ted trying to ruin the Crystal Palace? If so, why? And what, if anything, did all this have to do with Henry MacDonald's missing money?

Nancy looked at the clock on the wall. It was almost time for the women's programs to begin. Since this was the most popular event of the competition, it was also the most likely time for another act of sabotage.

But Ted wasn't even in the arena, Nancy reminded herself. And Pete—Brad Peters—could hardly show up at the Crystal Palace without arousing suspicions, now that he had been fired. Ted must be really sick to be away from the Crystal Palace today, Nancy thought.

Nancy gasped. With all that had happened today, she had completely forgotten—she had been parked next to Ted's car in the garage this morning! He *was* here. And Nancy would bet he was planning to carry out his nastiest surprise of all while everyone believed he was miles from the Crystal Palace, sick in bed.

Nancy slipped out of the office. She had to find Alison—quick! She froze as she saw a man walking briskly toward her. It was Ted.

Nancy was about to greet him and act as casual as possible. But suddenly the shrill beeping of an alarm filled the hallway. She heard shouts coming from the lobby: "Fire! Fire!"

# 15

## The Seventh Crystal

Nancy felt a hand on her shoulder. Ted was standing next to her, a gym bag in his hand.

"T-Ted . . ." she stammered. "I thought you were sick."

"I'm feeling much better," Ted replied, drawing his mouth into a thin smile. "Inconvenient time for a fire drill, isn't it?"

Nancy edged toward the end of the hallway, wondering whether Ted realized she suspected him. "I guess we'd better get out of here." She quickened her footsteps.

Ted stood in her path, holding out his hand to stop her. He watched her as Nancy took in the bandage stretched across his palm. "You're not going anywhere," he said firmly. "I've been keeping my eye on you."

Nancy glanced behind her. She heard shouts

and scuffling as the spectators evacuated the arena. Taking a deep breath, she told herself to stay calm.

"Alison was right," Ted said. "You're a great detective, Nancy Drew. But you know too much."

Nancy's heart pounded. "Thank you," she replied coolly, eyeing Ted's gym bag. Was there a weapon in there? What was he planning now?

"You could have ruined my plans big-time." Ted frowned at Nancy. "I'm glad I had the foresight to follow you every step of the way."

Nancy nodded slowly. "That day in the sculpture garden . . . you were tailing me, weren't you?"

"You don't think I wanted to be with *Meg*, do you?" A shadow crossed Ted's face. "She never looked at me twice until I got rich." He snorted. "And she thinks I don't have a clue she's been using me for my money."

Nancy watched Ted clench and unclench his fist. "So you decided to pay Meg back," she speculated. "You set her up." She ticked off the evidence on her fingers. "The eyedrops, the lipstick, the barrette . . . Meg's disagreements with Alison, which I'm sure you encouraged."

Ted nodded, seeming pleased with himself. "Not that I intended for Bess to be poisoned when I put the eyedrops in Kerri's drink. But it ended up working out nicely, if I do say so myself. And you obediently followed every clue I planted for

135

you. But now I'm afraid you're getting a little too close to the truth for your own good." His eyes bored into hers.

Realizing this was probably her only chance to escape, Nancy tried to dart past Ted. But he grabbed her arm and, with the iron grip of an athlete, propelled her back into Alison's office. The sound of the fire alarm grew faint when he locked the door behind them. He pointed to a chair and ordered Nancy to sit in it.

She sat and watched as Ted unzipped his gym bag and pulled out several skate laces knotted together. He quickly tied them around Nancy's hands and feet.

"Ted," Nancy said carefully, "I'm sure you realize how dangerous this situation is for both of us. The building could be on fire."

"I pulled the alarm." Ted smiled. "You don't think I'd set fire to such a beautiful building. I love the Crystal Palace."

"If you love the Crystal Palace, then why are you trying to ruin it?" Nancy asked.

Nancy gasped as Ted tugged hard on the laces around her wrists. "I would never ruin the Crystal Palace. Never, do you understand me? I'm trying to save it before *she* ruins it."

Ted was talking about Alison, Nancy realized with a start. That's why he was trying to spoil the competition. He was trying to drive Alison out of business and take the Crystal Palace away from her.

"Alison loves working with you, Ted," Nancy began carefully. "She's told me so several times. I'm sure if—"

"Alison's okay," Ted cut in quickly. "But she's just a kid. I've worked here fifteen years. She's got no business running an arena like this, calling me her assistant. She'll make the Crystal Palace an embarrassment to her uncle's good name."

"That's the last thing Alison wants to do," Nancy said.

"Then she should give up. She might be stubborn, but I'm going to make her an offer she won't be able to turn down."

Ted seemed to be looking through Nancy, a faraway expression on his face. "When I started working here, Henry told me if I did a good job, I might run this place someday." He shook his head. "Now I know he lied to me. Henry always planned to leave the Crystal Palace to his spoiled brat niece." Ted pounded his fist against Alison's desk. "But after I got my inheritance, I was just too close to let my dreams go up in smoke."

Nancy's eyes grew wide. "An arena this size must cost a few million dollars. You inherited that much money?"

"No. But I thought I knew how to get my hands on the rest of the funds I needed to buy the Crystal Palace." He scowled. "I just didn't bet on how well old Henry would hide his precious ice."

Precious ice? What was Ted talking about?

Ted smiled coldly at Nancy. "This is where

137

you're going to come in handy. You're such a good detective, you're going to find it for me." He breathed heavily as he pulled Nancy's chair in front of Alison's television set. "And then I can get rid of you permanently."

Nancy closed her eyes, chilled by Ted's words. She had to think. How could ice be valuable? Why would it be hidden, and why did Ted want her to find it? Nancy drew in a deep breath as it dawned on her.

"Ice" was slang for diamonds.

Uncle Henry must have invested the missing money in diamonds! He hid them, and now Ted was trying to find the gems so he could sell them and use the money to buy the arena from Alison.

Ted pulled a videocassette from his gym bag. The label on the case was marked with Alison's name.

"I cleaned out Henry's office before Alison arrived in Minneapolis," Ted explained. "That's when I found this tape."

"Which you stole," Nancy said.

Ted nodded. "Of course. If Alison knew about this video, my plan would never work."

"You stole Sarah's skating tape, too," Nancy said.

Ted shrugged. "I thought it might be Henry's."

"When you saw it was Sarah's, you ditched it."

Ted nodded. "I was afraid you'd realize I used my key to get in here, so I planted Amanda's screwdriver by the door to make it look as if somebody had picked the lock. Fooled you, didn't I?"

Noting Ted's pleased expression, Nancy decided she might get more information from Ted if she gave him the chance to gloat about how clever he'd been. And she could gain some time.

"You must have stolen some of Henry's other files, too," Nancy said. "Information about his personal investments and any other references to this tape. *And* parts of the repair records, so Alison wouldn't see that you wasted her money by having the same repairs done twice. That was a smart move," she told Ted. "It had me stumped."

Ted smiled. "Thank you. I figured, the more desperate Alison was for money, the faster she'd agree to sell the arena," he explained. "I knew Waterworks was going out of business, so nobody could ask any questions later about the repairs. Brad Peters is an old friend of mine. He was happy to hurry his father off to Florida and then pocket the money for repairing the pipes under the ice— even though there was nothing wrong with them, since they'd just been fixed last year."

"And it worked out so well, you decided to hire Brad to fix a few more things at the Crystal Palace," Nancy guessed. "All to make Alison break down and sell the place."

"I just threw a little money from my inheritance at him, and he was happy," Ted said.

"Then you recommended to Alison that we stay at the Excelsior, because you knew Brad could get into our room whenever he wanted to." Nancy shivered. That was a creepy thought.

"Yes. Wasn't I clever?" Ted fed the tape into the VCR. "Now enough of your twenty questions," he told Nancy. "Shut up and watch this." He fast-forwarded for a moment, then pressed the Play button.

Nancy saw a man's face fill the screen. He looked dignified and kindly, with silver hair and a mustache.

"My brother raised you well, Alison," Henry said. "I'm so proud of you. You've become an intelligent and extremely capable young lady, and I'm confident you are the perfect person to manage the Crystal Palace after I'm gone."

With a grunt of disgust, Ted turned his back on Nancy to press the Fast-forward button again. Nancy struggled to undo the ties that bound her hands, but the laces were knotted tightly.

"Okay, listen up," Ted said, removing his finger from the VCR button and glancing at her. She immediately stopped her struggling.

Henry was looking earnestly into the camera. "My accountants thought it was a crazy idea, but what do they know? At any rate, I kept my investment a secret from them—from everyone. But the diamonds are yours now, Alison. Sparkling gems, just as you are my sparkling gem. The diamonds are floating in the ice, Alison. Do you understand? Under the seventh crystal."

Uncle Henry's message was cut off as Ted

abruptly hit the Stop button on the VCR. "Float-ing in the ice," he repeated to Nancy. "I already looked under the ice when the pipes were being repaired. There weren't any diamonds there. I need you to think. What is the seventh crystal? Where are the diamonds?"

Nancy looked at the bare spot on the wall where the Monet print had hung before it was destroyed.

"I did some research on 'floating ice.' It was the name of that painting that I trashed." Ted sneered as he gestured to the empty space on the wall. "A lot of good it did me. The diamonds weren't there. And I didn't even manage to ruin the tires on the Zamboni with the broken glass, since you had to go and trip on the ice." He paused. "And then there's that sculpture, *The Six Crystals.* I asked the museum curator what the seventh crystal could mean. But he was no help."

*The Six Crystals,* Nancy thought, was Henry MacDonald's beloved bench sculpture. Her eyes strayed to the crystal sculpture on Alison's desk. The skating figure was his other cherished sculp-ture.

That must be the seventh crystal! Nancy was sure she had hit upon it! Floating in the ice under the seventh crystal were the diamonds. It had to be. Alison would know what her uncle Henry had meant by a seventh crystal. Her uncle had had the sculpture custom-made, and it was certainly large enough to hold precious gems. If Henry MacDon-ald was as fond of secret hiding places as Alison had said, maybe he'd had the sculpture made especially for that purpose.

There was a loud pounding on the door. "Fire Department!" a man's voice called.

Nancy opened her mouth to cry out when Ted clapped a hand over the lower half of her face. He grabbed Alison's wool scarf from a chair and used it as a gag, shoving it into her mouth.

Nancy continued to struggle, kicking the desk with her bound feet. If there were people out there, she had to make sure they heard her.

"Shut up!" Ted whispered fiercely. Desperate to silence her, he reached for the heavy crystal sculpture. As he raised it above her head, Nancy mustered all her strength to kick him in the shins.

Ted yelped in pain, and Nancy managed to duck away from the flying statue, which missed her head by inches. The sculpture smashed against the wall, shattering into pieces. Nancy watched as a cascade of diamonds spilled onto the carpeted floor.

# 16

## Gold Medal Performance

As Ted dived for the diamonds, Nancy heard a key turning in the lock. A moment later a firefighter burst into the office, followed by George and Bess.

For an instant Ted froze, and Nancy surprised him by kicking him mightily with her bound feet. George knocked him to the ground with a flying tackle. She and the firefighter held Ted pinned in place as Bess scrambled to pick up the scattered diamonds.

Within minutes Alison appeared with two of the police officers who had been guarding the arena. She finished untying Nancy as one of the officers handcuffed Ted.

The other cop took the diamonds from Bess. "We'll need these for evidence," he told Alison. "But they'll be returned to you as soon as possible."

Alison nodded numbly. "Thanks."

Ted stared at the ground in stony silence as a police officer led him out into the corridor.

"You'll have to come down to the station later to give a statement," the other officer told Nancy. "You're one lucky lady," he added.

"Tell me about it." Nancy looked at Bess and George. "How did you know I was in trouble?"

"I saw Ted sneaking around the rink," Bess explained. "I knew he was supposed to be out sick, so it seemed strange. And then the fire alarm went off."

"We looked for you everywhere outside, but we couldn't find you," George explained. "That's when we asked the fire department to check in here." She smiled. "Bess was very persuasive. She talked them into letting us come inside, too."

"After all, the fire was a false alarm, and we would have found you eventually," the firefighter told Nancy. "We were making rounds of the entire building, but we started on the other side."

Nancy glanced over at Alison, who had returned from the utility closet with a broom, still looking slightly dazed.

"It's pretty hard to believe Ted did all those terrible things, isn't it?" Nancy asked her.

Alison nodded. "Ted's been a good friend since I was a little girl. I trusted him completely." She bent to sweep the broken fragments of the sculpture into a dustpan.

"I'm sorry things turned out this way," Nancy said.

Alison smiled. "Don't be. I know there are still people I can trust in this world. Like you." She hugged Nancy and said, "Thank you for everything."

On Sunday evening Nancy, Bess, and George applauded as Kerri stepped up to the podium, followed by Dominique Morrow, then Sarah. Sarah beamed as the gold medal was placed around her neck. Kerri barely mustered a smile as she was awarded the bronze.

"Way to go, Sarah!" Meg shouted. She, Amanda, and Scott were in the seats in front of Nancy's group.

Amanda put two fingers in her mouth and whistled. She turned around in her seat and asked the others, "Wasn't Sarah sensational? Her long program tonight was even better than her short."

Bess nodded.

"She definitely deserved to win," George said, and Nancy agreed.

The women's medalists returned to the stands. Scott gave Sarah a big hug and kiss on the cheek, his eyes shining with pride.

"You were right all along," Scott admitted to his coach. "I am totally in awe of how good Sarah is. And she's so much better since she cut back on her pairs practice time."

"She would improve even more if she did as I asked and gave up pairs entirely," Meg said, a twinkle in her eye as she looked at Sarah.

Sarah put an arm around Scott. "I know." She gently touched the Ace bandage on her leg. "I got this injury practicing with Scott. I was too ashamed to tell you the truth, Meg."

"So was all the sneaking around worth it?" Meg asked her.

Sarah shook her head. "No. I was being petty and selfish, and I was holding back Scott and Amanda from doing their best." She squeezed Scott's hand. "After watching this competition, I know that Choi and Ogden are going to be a hundred times better than Phillips and Ogden ever were." She smiled at Amanda. "I'm sorry for the way I acted. And I'm so proud of you guys for coming in second. Your long program was awesome!"

"Thanks." Amanda blushed. "I'm sorry, too, Sarah. After everything that's happened this week, I've learned an important lesson. I know how much Scott cares for you. And I promise I'll never try to come between you again."

Sarah embraced Amanda. "No hard feelings?"

"No hard feelings," Amanda said lightly. "I'm going to go congratulate Dominique, okay?"

Sarah watched as Amanda threaded her way across the bleachers, keeping her head down as she passed a pouting Kerri.

146

Alison hurried over from the judges' table to congratulate Meg and Sarah.

"Congratulations to you, too, Alison." Meg reached out her hand. "You did an excellent job staging this competition under extraordinarily difficult circumstances."

Alison smiled. "Are we ready to bury the hatchet?"

"I think so." Meg looked down at the ground. "Ted really had me believing you were a terrible person. I can't imagine why I was stupid enough to listen to him."

"Ted had a lot of us fooled," Alison said quietly. She turned to Sarah. "Hey, Sarah, let me see that gorgeous gold medal of yours."

Sarah lifted it over her head and handed it to Alison. Everyone crowded around her to admire it.

"I may be the one who won this medal," Sarah said, "but we all know who the real hero of this competition is." She took Nancy's hand and held it high in the air as everyone cheered.

Alison smiled at Nancy. "Sarah's right. I think you deserve a medal for your dazzling performance on this case."

Nancy grinned. "I'd be happy if I could learn to skate without falling on my face."

"Maybe you can't skate like the pros, but what you did off the ice made it possible to keep the skaters on the ice. And it kept my uncle's dream

147

alive," Alison said. "I'll never forget what you've done. And as a very small token of my appreciation . . ."

Motioning for Amanda to join them, Alison beckoned to a snack bar waiter, who led them all to a table that held a cake decorated to look like a gold medal. "Thank you and congratulations, everyone," Alison said.

"I'm glad I gave up my diet," Bess murmured as she took a thick slice. Then she licked yellow frosting from her fingers.

Alison cleared her throat. She lifted a mug of hot chocolate. "I'd like to propose a toast. To us. May our futures always hold the happiness and success that we've found here tonight." Her eyes filled with tears. "And to my uncle Henry."

Nancy clinked her mug against Alison's. "To Uncle Henry."

"And especially to Nancy," Alison said, "for being a total pro and a great friend."

# NANCY DREW® MYSTERY STORIES  By Carolyn Keene

| | | |
|---|---|---|
| ☐ | #58: THE FLYING SAUCER MYSTERY | 72320-0/$3.99 |
| ☐ | #62: THE KACHINA DOLL MYSTERY | 67220-7/$3.99 |
| ☐ | #68: THE ELUSIVE HEIRESS | 62478-4/$3.99 |
| ☐ | #72: THE HAUNTED CAROUSEL | 66227-9/$3.99 |
| ☐ | #73: ENEMY MATCH | 64283-9/$3.50 |
| ☐ | #77: THE BLUEBEARD ROOM | 66857-9/$3.50 |
| ☐ | #79: THE DOUBLE HORROR OF FENLEY PLACE | 64387-8/$3.99 |
| ☐ | #81: MARDI GRAS MYSTERY | 64961-2/$3.99 |
| ☐ | #83: THE CASE OF THE VANISHING VEIL | 63413-5/$3.99 |
| ☐ | #84: THE JOKER'S REVENGE | 63414-3/$3.99 |
| ☐ | #85: THE SECRET OF SHADY GLEN | 63416-X/$3.99 |
| ☐ | #87: THE CASE OF THE RISING STAR | 66312-7/$3.99 |
| ☐ | #89: THE CASE OF THE DISAPPEARING DEEJAY | 66314-3/$3.99 |
| ☐ | #91: THE GIRL WHO COULDN'T REMEMBER | 66316-X/$3.99 |
| ☐ | #92: THE GHOST OF CRAVEN COVE | 66317-8/$3.99 |
| ☐ | #93: THE CASE OF THE SAFECRACKER'S SECRET | 66318-6/$3.99 |
| ☐ | #94: THE PICTURE-PERFECT MYSTERY | 66319-4/$3.99 |
| ☐ | #96: THE CASE OF THE PHOTO FINISH | 69281-X/$3.99 |
| ☐ | #97: THE MYSTERY AT MAGNOLIA MANSION | 69282-8/$3.99 |
| ☐ | #98: THE HAUNTING OF HORSE ISAND | 69284-4/$3.99 |
| ☐ | #99: THE SECRET AT SEVEN ROCKS | 69285-2/$3.99 |
| ☐ | #101: THE MYSTERY OF THE MISSING MILLIONAIRES | 69287-9/$3.99 |
| ☐ | #102: THE SECRET IN THE DARK | 69279-8/$3.99 |
| ☐ | #103: THE STRANGER IN THE SHADOWS | 73049-5/$3.99 |
| ☐ | #104: THE MYSTERY OF THE JADE TIGER | 73050-9/$3.99 |
| ☐ | #105: THE CLUE IN THE ANTIQUE TRUNK | 73051-7/$3.99 |
| ☐ | #107: THE LEGEND OF MINER'S CREEK | 73053-3/$3.99 |
| ☐ | #109: THE MYSTERY OF THE MASKED RIDER | 73055-X/$3.99 |
| ☐ | #110: THE NUTCRACKER BALLET MYSTERY | 73056-8/$3.99 |
| ☐ | #111: THE SECRET AT SOLAIRE | 79297-0/$3.99 |
| ☐ | #112: CRIME IN THE QUEEN'S COURT | 79298-9/$3.99 |
| ☐ | #113: THE SECRET LOST AT SEA | 79299-7/$3.99 |
| ☐ | #114: THE SEARCH FOR THE SILVER PERSIAN | 79300-4/$3.99 |
| ☐ | #115: THE SUSPECT IN THE SMOKE | 79301-2/$3.99 |
| ☐ | #116: THE CASE OF THE TWIN TEDDY BEARS | 79302-0/$3.99 |
| ☐ | #117: MYSTERY ON THE MENU | 79303-9/$3.99 |
| ☐ | #118: TROUBLE AT LAKE TAHOE | 79304-7/$3.99 |
| ☐ | #119: THE MYSTERY OF THE MISSING MASCOT | 87202-8/$3.99 |
| ☐ | #120: THE CASE OF THE FLOATING CRIME | 87203-6/$3.99 |
| ☐ | #121: THE FORTUNE-TELLER'S SECRET | 87204-4/$3.99 |
| ☐ | #122: THE MESSAGE IN THE HAUNTED MANSION | 87205-2/$3.99 |
| ☐ | #123: THE CLUE ON THE SILVER SCREEN | 87206-0/$3.99 |
| ☐ | #124: THE SECRET OF THE SCARLET HAND | 87207-9/$3.99 |
| ☐ | #125: THE TEEN MODEL MYSTERY | 87208-7/$3.99 |
| ☐ | #126: THE RIDDLE IN THE RARE BOOK | 87209-5/$3.99 |
| ☐ | #127: THE CASE OF THE DANGEROUS SOLUTION | 50500-9/$3.99 |
| ☐ | #128: THE TREASURE IN THE ROYAL TOWER | 50502-5/$3.99 |
| ☐ | #129: THE BABYSITTER BURGLARIES | 50507-6/$3.99 |
| ☐ | #130: THE SIGN OF THE FALCON | 50508-4/$3.99 |
| ☐ | #131: THE HIDDEN INHERITANCE | 50509-2/$3.99 |
| ☐ | #132: THE FOX HUNT MYSTERY | 50510-6/$3.99 |
| ☐ | #133: THE MYSTERY AT THE CRYSTAL PALACE | 50515-7/$3.99 |
| ☐ | NANCY DREW GHOST STORIES - #1 | 69132-5/$3.99 |

## A MINSTREL® BOOK
### Published by Pocket Books

---

**Simon & Schuster, Mail Order Dept. HB5, 200 Old Tappan Rd., Old Tappan, N.J. 07675**
Please send me copies of the books checked. Please add appropriate local sales tax.
☐ Enclosed full amount per copy with this coupon (Send check or money order only)
☐ If order is $10.00 or more, you may charge to one of the following accounts:  ☐ Mastercard  ☐ Visa
Please be sure to include proper postage and handling: 0.95 for first copy; 0.50 for each additional copy ordered.

Name _____

Address _____

City _____  State/Zip _____

Credit Card # _____  Exp.Date _____

Signature _____

Books listed are also available at your bookstore.  Prices are subject to change without notice.

760-21